*Letters From
Father Christmas*

J.R.R. TOLKIEN

Letters From Father Christmas

Edited by Baillie Tolkien

HarperCollins*Publishers*

HarperCollins*Publishers*
77–85 Fulham Palace Road,
Hammersmith, London W6 8JB

www.tolkien.co.uk

This paperback edition 2012
1

First published by George Allen & Unwin 1976
Based on the edition first published by HarperCollins*Publishers* 1999,
revised 2004

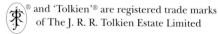
All illustrated material in this book reproduced
courtesy of The Bodleian Library, University of Oxford
and selected from their holdings labelled MS Tolkien
Drawings 36–68; 83, folios 1–65; and 89, folio 18

ISBN 978 0 00 746337 4

Introduction

To the children of J. R. R. Tolkien, the interest and importance of Father Christmas extended beyond his filling of their stockings on Christmas Eve; for he wrote a letter to them every year, in which he described in words and pictures his house, his friends, and the events, hilarious or alarming, at the North Pole. The first of the letters came in 1920, when John, the eldest, was three years old; and for over twenty years, through the childhoods of the three other children, Michael, Christopher and Priscilla, they continued to arrive each Christmas. Sometimes the envelopes, dusted with snow and bearing Polar postage stamps, were found in the house on the morning after his visit; sometimes the postman brought them; and the letters that the children wrote themselves vanished from the fireplace when no one was about.

As time went on, Father Christmas' household became larger, and whereas at first little is heard of anyone else except the North Polar Bear, later on there appear Snow-elves, Red Gnomes, Snow-men, Cave-bears, and the Polar Bear's nephews, Paksu and Valkotukka, who came on a visit and never went away. But the Polar Bear remained Father Christmas' chief assistant, and the chief cause of the disasters that led to muddles and deficiencies in the Christmas stockings; and sometimes he wrote on the letters his comments in angular capitals.

Eventually Father Christmas took on as his secretary an Elf named Ilbereth, and in the later letters Elves play an important part in the defence of Father Christmas' house and store-cellars against attacks by Goblins.

In this book are presented numerous examples of Father Christmas' shaky handwriting, and almost all the pictures that he sent are here reproduced; also included is the alphabet that the Polar Bear devised from the Goblin drawings on the walls of the caves where he was lost, and the letter that he sent to the children written in it.

FROM FATHER • CHRISTMAS

ME

FC

MY HOUSE

FC

Christmas House
NORTH POLE
1920

Love to
daddy, mummy,
michael & aunt-e
& mary

Dear John

I heard you ask daddy
what I was like & where
I lived. I have drawn
ME & My House for you.
Take care of the picture.
I am just off now for
Oxford with my bundle
of toys — some for you.
Hope I shall arrive in
time: the snow is very
thick at the NORTH POLE
tonight : Yr loving Fr. Chr.

1920

Christmas House,
North Pole
22nd December 1920

Dear John

I heard you ask daddy what I was like and where I
lived. I have drawn me and my house for you. Take
care of the picture. I am just off now for Oxford
with my bundle of toys – some for you. Hope I shall
arrive in time: the snow is very thick at the North Pole
tonight. Your loving Father Christmas

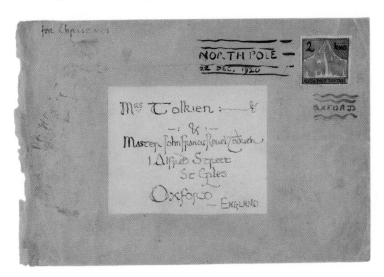

DEC. 23
1923

NORTH • POLE

POST

Master John Francis Tolkien
11. St Marks Terrace
Woodhouse Lane
Leeds

10

1923

North Pole
Christmas Eve: 1923

My dear John,

It is very cold today and my hand is very shaky –
I am nineteen hundred and twenty four, no! seven!
years old on Christmas Day, – lots older than your
great-grandfather, so I can't stop the pen wobbling,
but I hear that you are getting so good at reading that
I expect you will be able to read my letter.

I send you lots of love (and lots for Michael too) and
Lotts Bricks too (which are called that because there
are lots more for you to have next year if you let me
know in good time). I think they are prettier and
stronger and tidier than Picabrix. So I hope you will
like them.

Now I must go; it is a lovely fine night and I have got
hundreds of miles to go before morning – there is
such a lot to do.

A cold kiss from
Father Nicholas Christmas

Christmas Eve : 1923

North Pole

My dear John

It is very cold to day and
my hand is very shaky
I am nineteen hundred and twenty
no! seven!
four years old on Christmas day,
& is older than your great-grandfather,
so I can't stop the pen wobbling,
but I hear that you are getting
so good at reading that I expect
you will be able to read my letter

I send you lots of love (and lots for
Michael too) and Lots Brick too
(which are called that because there
are lots more for you to have next year
if you let me know in good time)
I think they are prettier and stronger
and tidier than Peabrix, so I hope
you will like them. Now I
must go; it is a lovely fine night
and I have got hundreds of miles
to go before morning — there is such
a lot to do. A cold kiss from
Fr. Nicholas Christmas

Dec 23. 1924

Michael Hilary

with love
from
Father, Christmas
I am
very busy this year: no
time for letter. Lots of
love. Hope the engine
goes well. Take care
of it. A big kiss

14

1924

Dear Michael Hilary

I am very busy this year: No time for letter. Lots of love.
Hope the engine goes well. Take care of it. A big kiss.

with love from
Father Christmas

December 23rd 1924

Dear John

Hope you have a happy Christmas. Only time for a short letter, my sleigh is waiting. Lots of new stockings to fill this year. Hope you will like station and things. A big kiss.

with love from
Father Christmas

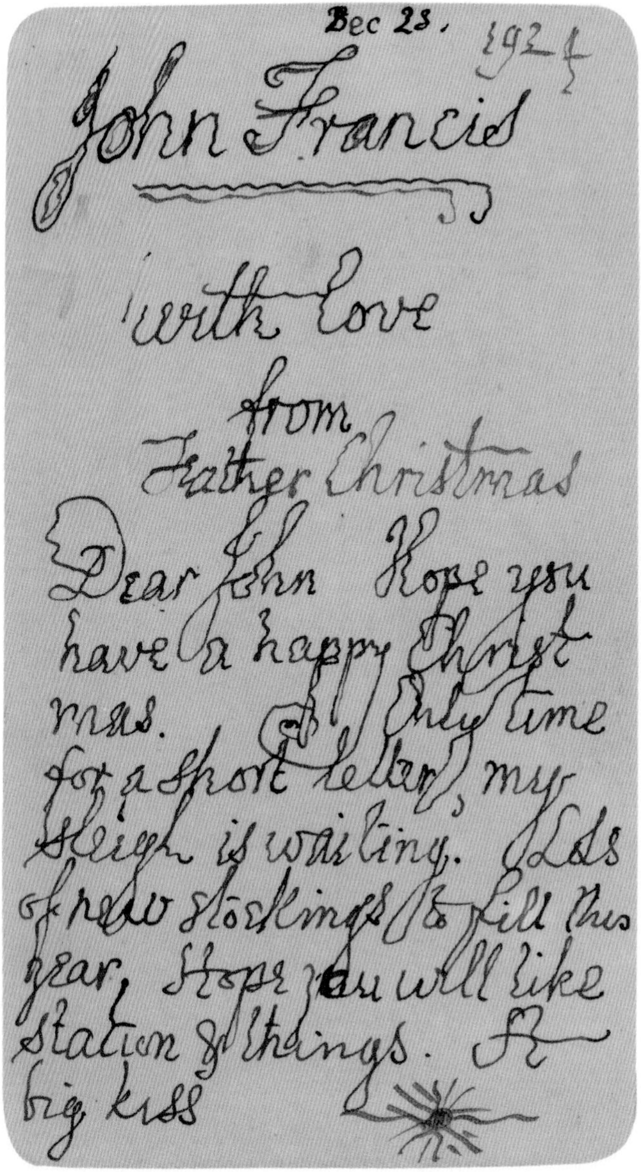
Dec 23. 1920

John Francis

with love
from
Father Christmas

Dear John Hope you have a happy Christmas. Only time for a short letter, my sleigh is waiting. Lots of new stockings to fill this year. Hope you will like station & things. A big kiss

Cliff House +
Top of the world
Near the North Pole

My dear boys

I am dreadfully busy this year—it makes my hand more shaky than ever when I think of it—and not very rich: in fact awful things have been happening, and some of the pres ents have got spoilt, and I haven't got the North Polar bear to help me, and I have had to move house just before Christmas, so you can imagine what a state everything is in, and you will see why I have a new address, and why I can write only one letter between you both. It all happened like this: one very windy day last November my hood blew off and went and stuck on the top of the North Pole. I told him not to, but the N.P. Bear climbed up to the thin top to get it down—and he did. The pole broke in the middle, and fell on the roof of my house and the N.P. Bear fell through the hole it made into the dining-room with my hood over his nose, and all the snow fell off the roof into the house and melted and put out all the fires and ran down into the cellars where I was collecting this year's presents, and the N.P. Bear's leg got broken. He is well again now, but I was so cross with him that he says he won't try to help me again. I expect his temper is hurt, and will be mended by next Christmas. I send you a picture of the accident, and of my new house on the cliffs above the N.P. with beautiful cellars in the cliffs. If John can't read my old shaky writing (1925 years old) he must get his father to. When is Michael going to learn to read, and write his own letters to me? Lots of love to you both and Christopher, whose name is rather like mine.

That's all. Goodbye. Father Christmas

1925

Cliff House,
Top of the World,
Near the North Pole
Christmas 1925

My dear boys,

I am dreadfully busy this year – it makes my hand
more shaky than ever when I think of it – and not
very rich; in fact awful things have been happening,

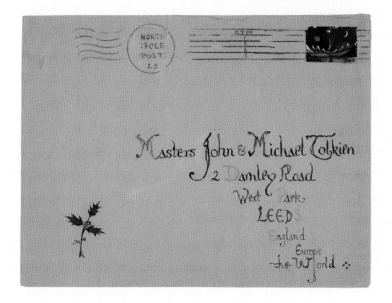

and some of the presents have got spoilt, and I haven't got the North Polar bear to help me, and I have had to move house just before Christmas, so you can imagine what a state everything is in, and you will see why I have a new address, and why I can only write one letter between you both.

It all happened like this: one very windy day last November my hood blew off and went and stuck on the top of the North Pole. I told him not to, but the North Polar Bear climbed up to the thin top to get it down – and he did. The pole broke in the middle and fell on the roof of my house, and the North Polar Bear fell through the hole it made into the dining room with my hood over his nose, and all the snow fell off the roof into the house and melted and put out all the fires and ran down into the cellars, where I was collecting this year's presents, and the North Polar Bear's leg got broken.

He is well again now, but I was so cross with him that he says he won't try to help me again – I expect his temper is hurt, and will be mended by next Christmas.

I send you a picture of the accident and of my new house on the cliffs above the North Pole (with beautiful cellars in the cliffs). If John can't read my old shaky writing (one thousand nine hundred and twenty-five years old) he must get his father to.

P.S.

me

FR Christmas was
in great hurry — told
me to put in one of his
magic wishing crackers.
As you pull, wish, & see
if it doesn't come true.
Excuse thick writing
I have a fat paw.
I help Fr. C. with his
packing: I live with
him. I am the

GREAT (Polar) BEAR

When is Michael going to learn to read, and write his own letters to me? Lots of love to you both and Christopher, whose name is rather like mine.

That's all: Good Bye
Father Christmas

P. S.

Father Christmas was in a great hurry – told me to put in one of his magic wishing crackers. As you pull, wish, and see if it doesn't come true. Excuse thick writing I have a fat paw. I help Father Christmas with his packing: I live with him. I am the GREAT (Polar) BEAR

1926

Cliff House,
Top of the World,
Near the North Pole
Monday December 20th 1926

My dear boys,

I am more shaky than usual this year. The North Polar
Bear's fault! It was the biggest bang in the world, and
the most monstrous firework there ever has been. It
turned the North Pole BLACK and shook all the stars
out of place, broke the moon into four – and the Man
in it fell into my back garden. He ate quite a lot of my
Christmas chocolates before he said he felt better and
climbed back to mend it and get the stars tidy.

Then I found out that the reindeer had broken loose.
They were running all over the country, breaking
reins and ropes and tossing presents up in the air.
They were all packed up to start, you see – yes it
only happened this morning: it was a sleighload of
chocolate things, which I always send to England
early. I hope yours are not badly damaged.

Christmas
1926

Cliff House
Top of the World
Near the NORTH POLE
Monday Dec 1926 20th

My dear boys,

I am more shaky than usual this year. The North Polar Bear's fault! It was the biggest bang in the world, & the most monstrous firework there ever has been. It turned the North Pole BLACK & shook all the stars out of place, broke the moon into four — and the Man in it fell into my back garden. He ate quite a lot of my Xmas chocolate before he said he felt better & climbed back to mend it and get the stars tidy. Then I found out that the reindeer had broken loose. They were running all over the country, breaking reins and ropes & dragging presents out in the air. They were all packed up to start, you see: — yes it only happened this morning: it was a sleighload of chocolate things which I always send to England early. I hope yours are not badly damaged. But isn't the N.P.B. silly? And he isn't a bit sorry! Of course he did it — you remember I had some last year because of him? The tap for turning on the Rory Bory Aylis fireworks is still in the cellar of my old house. The N.P.B. knew he must never never touch it. I only let it off on special days like Christmas. He says he thought it was cut off since we moved — anyway he was nosing round the ruins this morning soon after breakfast (he hides things to eat there) and turned on all the Northern Lights for two years in one go. You have never heard or seen anything like it. I have tried to draw a picture of it; but I am too shaky to do it properly and you can't paint fizzing light can you?

I think the PB has spoilt the picture rather — of course he can't draw with these great fat paws — by going and putting a bit of his own in about me chasing the reindeer and him laughing. He did laugh. So did I when I saw him

hide. NPB
I can — and write
without shaking

PTO

trying to draw reindeer, and making his nose white year—

FATHER X. had to hurry away and leave me to finish. He is old and gets worried when funny things happen. You would have laughed too! I think it is good of me laughing! It was a lovely firework. The reindeer will run quick to England this year. They are still frightened! ⟶

I must go and help pack. I don't know what F.C. would do without me. He always forgets what a lot of packing I do for him. ⟶

The Snow Man is addressing our envelopes this year. He is F.C.'s gardener — but we don't get much but snowdrops and frost-ferns to grow here. He always writes in white, just with his finger. ⟶

A merry Christmas to you from . NPB .

And love from Father Christmas to you all.

26

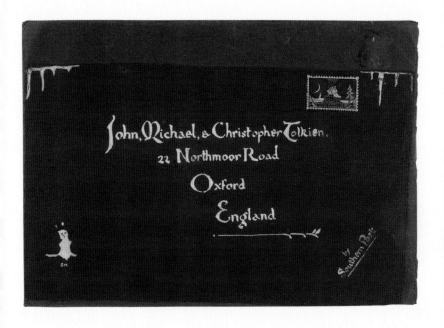

But isn't the North Polar Bear silly? And he isn't a
bit sorry! Of course he did it – you remember I had
to move last year because of him? The tap for turning
on the Rory Bory Aylis fireworks is still in the cellar
of my old house. The North Polar Bear knew he must
never, never touch it. I only let it off on special days
like Christmas. He says he thought it was cut off since
we moved.

Anyway, he was nosing round the ruins this morning
soon after breakfast (he hides things to eat there)
and turned on all the Northern Lights for two years
in one go. You have never heard or seen anything like
it. I have tried to draw a picture of it; but I am too

shaky to do it properly and you can't paint fizzing light can you?

I think the Polar Bear has spoilt the picture rather – of course he can't draw with those great fat paws –

Rude! I can – and write without shaking.

by going and putting a bit of his own about me chasing the reindeer and him laughing. He did laugh too. So did I when I saw him trying to draw reindeer, and inking his nice white paws.

Father Christmas had to hurry away and leave me to finish. He is old and gets worried when funny things happen. You would have laughed too! I think it is good of me laughing. It was a lovely firework. The reindeer will run quick to England this year. They are still frightened!...

I must go and help pack. I don't know what Father Christmas would do without me. He always forgets what a lot of packing I do for him...

The Snow Man is addressing our envelopes this year. He is Father Christmas's gardener – but we don't get much but snowdrops and frost-ferns to grow here. He always writes in white, just with his finger...

A merry Christmas to you from North Polar Bear

And love from Father Christmas to you all.

29

Cliff House
Top o' the World
near the
North Pole

Wednesday December 21st 1927

My dear people:— John, Michael, Christopher, also Maud, also Mummy, also Auntie Jennie — also Daddy, there seem to get more & more of you every year & I get busier & busier: still I hope that I have managed to bring you all something you wanted, though not everything you asked for (Michael & Christopher!). I haven't heard from John this year, I suppose — he is growing too big and won't soon hang up his stocking soon! It has been so bitter at the N.P. lately that the N.P.B. (you know who I mean?) has spent most of the time asleep and has been less use than usual this Xmas. The world became colder than any cold thing ever has been & when the N.P.B. put his nose against it took the skin off, that is why it is bandaged with red flannel in the picture (but the bandage has slipped). Why did he? I don't know, but he is always putting his nose where it ought to be — into my cupboards for instance.

Also it has been very dark here since winter began. We haven't seen the Sun, of course, for three months (but there are Northern lights this year — you remember the awful accident last year? There will be none again until the end of 1928. The N.P.B. has got his cousin (and distant friend) the GREAT BEAR to shine extra bright for us and this week I have hired a comet to do my packing by, but it doesn't work as well — you can see that by my picture. The North Polar Bear has not really been any more sensible this year: yesterday he was snowballing the Snow Man in the garden & pushed him over the edge of the cliff so that he fell into my sleigh at the bottom & broke lots of things — one of them was himself, used some. So what was left of him to paint my white picture. We shall have to make ourselves a new gardener when we are less busy.

The MAN in the MOON paid me a visit the other day — a fortnight ago exactly December 7th — he often does about this time — as he gets lonely in the Moon, and we make him a nice little plum pudding (he is so fond of things with plums in). His fingers were cold as usual & the N.P.B. made him play "snapdragons" to warm them. Of course he burnt them & then he licked them, and then he liked the brandy, and then the Bear gave him lots more, and he went fast asleep on the sofa. Then I went down into the cellars to make crackers, and he rolled off the sofa and the wicked bear pushed him underneath & forgot all about him! He can never be away a whole night from the moon; but he was this time. Suddenly the Snow Man (he wasn't broken then) rushed in out of the garden, next day just after teatime, and said the moon was going out! The dragons had come out & were making an awful smoke and smother. We rolled him out and shook him & he simply whizzed back, but it was ages before he got things quite cleared up.

1927

Cliff House,
Top o'the World,
near the North Pole
Wednesday December 21st 1927

My dear people: there seem to get more and more of you every year.

I get poorer and poorer: still I hope that I have managed to bring you all something you wanted, though not everything you asked for (Michael and

Christopher! I haven't heard from John this year.
I suppose he is growing too big and won't even
hang up his stocking soon).

It has been so bitter at the North Pole lately that the
North Polar Bear has spent most of the time asleep
and has been less use than usual this Christmas.

**Everybody does sleep most of the time here in winter –
especially Father Christmas.**

The North Pole became colder than any cold thing
ever has been, and when the North Polar Bear put
his nose against it – it took the skin off: now it is
bandaged with red flannel. Why did he? I don't know,
but he is always putting his nose where it oughtn't to
be – into my cupboards for instance.

That's because I am hungry

Also it has been very dark here since winter began. We
haven't seen the Sun, of course, for three months, but
there are no Northern Lights this year – you remember
the awful accident last year? There will be none again
until the end of 1928. The North Polar Bear has got
his cousin (and distant friend) the Great Bear to shine
extra bright for us, and this week I have hired a comet
to do my packing by, but it doesn't work as well.

The North Polar Bear has not really been any more
sensible this year:

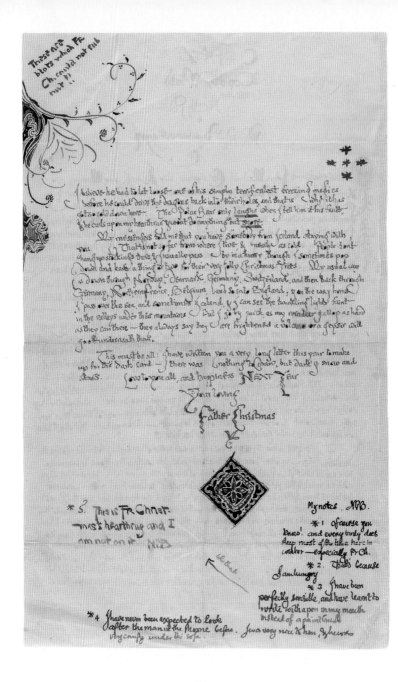

These are Fr Xmas's blots which Ch. could not rub out !!

I believe he had to let loose out of his simple terrifi-enlest freezing magics before he could drive the dragons back into their holes, and that is why it was extra cold down here. The Polar Bear only laughs when I tell him it his fault, & he curls up on my hearthrug & won't do anything but snore.

My messengers tell me that you have somebody from Iceland staying with you. That's not so far from where I live & nearly as cold. People don't hang up stockings there I usually pass – or anyway though I sometimes pop down and leave a thing or two for their very jolly Christmas Trees. My usual way is down through Norway, Denmark, Germany, Switzerland, and then back through Germany, Northern France, Belgium, land so into England, & on the way home I pass over the sea, and sometimes I Iceland. & I can see the twinkling lights faint in the valleys under their mountains – But I go very quick, as my reindeer gallop as hard as they can there – they always say they are frightened a volcano or a geysir will go off underneath them.

This must be all: I have written you a very long letter this year to make up for the dark card – & there was I nothing to draw, but dark & snow and stars. Love to you all, and happiness NEXT year.

Your loving

Father Christmas

* 5. This is Fr Christmas's hearthrug and I am not on it NPB

the Bear ↑

My notes. NPB.
* 1 Of course you know! and every body does sleep most of the time here in winter – especially Fr Ch.
* 2. That's because I am hungry
* 3 I have been perfectly sensible and have learnt to write with a pen in my mouth instead of a paintbrush. I was very nice when I heard

* 4 I have never been expected to look after the man in the Moone before. I was comfy under the sofa.

I have been perfectly sensible, and have learnt to write with a pen in my mouth instead of a paintbrush.

Yesterday he was snowballing the Snow Man in the garden and pushed him over the edge of the cliff so that he fell into my sleigh at the bottom and broke lots of things – one of them was himself. I used some of what was left of him to paint my white picture. We shall have to make ourselves a new gardener when we are less busy.

The Man in the Moon paid me a visit the other day – a fortnight ago exactly – he often does about this time, as he gets lonely in the Moon, and we make him a nice little Plum Pudding (he is so fond of things with plums in!)

His fingers were cold as usual, and the North Polar Bear made him play 'snapdragons' to warm them. Of course he burnt them, and then he licked them, and then he liked the brandy, and then the Bear gave him lots more, and he went fast asleep on the sofa. Then I went down into the cellars to make crackers, and he rolled off the sofa, and the wicked bear pushed him underneath and forgot all about him! He can never be away a whole night from the moon; but he was this time.

I have never been expected to look after the Man in the Moon before. I was very nice to him, and he was very comfy under the sofa.

Suddenly the Snow Man (he wasn't broken then) rushed in out of the garden, next day just after teatime, and said the moon was going out! The dragons had come out and were making an awful smoke and smother. We rolled him out and shook him and he simply whizzed back, but it was ages before he got things quite cleared up.

I believe he had to let loose one of his simply terrificalest freezing magics before he could drive the dragons back into their holes, and that is why it has got so cold down here.

The Polar Bear only laughs when I tell him it's his fault, and he curls up on my hearthrug and won't do anything but snore.

My messengers told me that you have somebody from Iceland staying with you. That is not so far from where I live, and nearly as cold. People don't hang up stockings there, and I usually pass by in a hurry, though I sometimes pop down and leave a thing or two for their very jolly Christmas Trees.

My usual way is down through Norway, Denmark, Germany, Switzerland, and then back through Germany, Northern France, Belgium, and so into England: and on the way home I pass over the sea, and sometimes Iceland and I can see the twinkling lights faint in the valleys under their mountains. But I go by quick, as my reindeer gallop as hard as they can there – they always say they are frightened a volcano or a geyser will go off underneath them.

This must be all: I have written you a very long letter this year as there was nothing to draw, but dark and snow and stars.

Love to you all, and happiness next year.

Your loving Father Christmas

1928

Top o' the World,
North Pole
Thursday December 20th 1928

My dear boys,

Another Christmas and I am another year older –
and so are you. I feel quite well all the same – very
nice of Michael to ask – and not quite so shaky.
But that is because we have got all the lighting and
heating right again after the cold dark year we had
in 1927 – you remember about it?

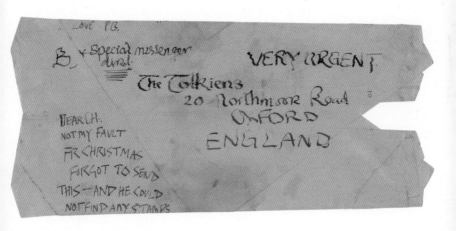

LOVE PB.

B. × Special messenger
dircl.

VERY URGENT

The Tolkiens
20 Northmoor Road
OXFORD
ENGLAND

DEAR CH.
NOT MY FAULT
FIR CHRISTMAS
FORGOT TO SEND
THIS – AND HE COULD
NOT FIND ANY STAMPS

My Dear Boys ....

ANOTHER CHRISTMAS and I am another year
older—and so are you. I feel quite well all the same—very nice
of MICHAEL to ask—and not quite so shaky. But that is because we have got all the lighting and heating right again after
the cold dark year we had in 1927—you remember about it?
And I expect you remember whose fault it was? What do
you think the poor dear old bear has been and done this time?
Nothing as bad as letting off all the lights. Only fell from top to
bottom of the main stairs on Thursday! We were beginning
to get the first lot of parcels down out of the storerooms into the
hall. PB would insist on taking an enormous pile on his
head as well as lots in his arms. Bang Rumble Clatter Crash!
awful moanings and growlings: I ran out on to the landing and saw
he had fallen from top to bottom onto his nose—leaving a trail of balls
bundles parcels & things all the way down—and he had fallen on top of
some and smashed them. I hope you got none of these by accident?
I have drawn you a picture of it all. PB was rather grumpy at my
drawing it: he says my Christmas pictures always make fun of him
& that one year he will send one drawn by himself of me being idiotic
(but of course I never am, and he can't draw well enough). He
joggled my arm and spoilt the little picture at the bottom of the moon

WHO
LEFT THE
SOAP
ON THE
STAIRS?
NOT I!!!

OF COURSE
NATURALLY

YES I CAN
I DREW
FLAG
AT
END.

38

And I expect you remember whose fault it was?
What do you think the poor dear old bear has been
and done this time? Nothing as bad as letting off all
the lights. Only fell from top to bottom of the main
stairs on Thursday!

Who'd left the soap on the stairs? Not me!

We were beginning to get the first lot of parcels down
out of the storerooms into the hall. Polar Bear would
insist on taking an enormous pile on his head as well
as lots in his arms. Bang Rumble Clatter Crash! Awful
moanings and growlings.

I ran out on to the landing and saw he had fallen
from top to bottom on to his nose leaving a trail of
balls, bundles, parcels and things all the way down –
and he had fallen on top of some and smashed them.
I hope you got none of these by accident? I have
drawn you a picture of it all. Polar Bear was rather
grumpy at my drawing it:

Of course, naturally.

He says my Christmas pictures always make fun of
him and that one year he will send one drawn by
himself of me being idiotic (but of course I never
am, and he can't draw well enough).

Yes I can. I drew the flag at the end.

He joggled my arm and spoilt the little picture at the bottom of the moon laughing and Polar Bear shaking his fist at it.

When he had picked himself up he ran out of doors and wouldn't help clear up because I sat on the stairs and laughed as soon as I found there was not much damage done – that is why the moon smiled: but the part showing Polar Bear angry was cut off because he smudged it.

But anyway I thought you would like a picture of the inside of my new big house for a change. The chief hall is under the largest dome, where we pile the presents usually ready to load on the sleighs at the doors. Polar Bear and I built it nearly all ourselves, and laid all the blue and mauve tiles. The banisters and roof are not quite straight…

Not my fault. Father Christmas did the banisters.

…but it doesn't really matter. I painted the pictures on the walls of the trees and stars and suns and moons. Then I said to Polar Bear, "I shall leave the frieze (F. R. I. E. Z. E.) to you."

He said, "I should have thought there was enough freeze outside – and your colours inside, all purply-grey-y-bluey-pale greeny are cold enough too."

I said, "Don't be a silly bear: do your best, there's a good old polar" – and what a result!! Icicles all round

laughing and PB shaking his fist at it. When he had picked himself up he ran out of doors & would'nt help clear up because I
sat on the stairs and laughed as soon as I found there was not much
damage done — that is why the moon smiled : as you can see, but the
part showing PB angry was cut off because he smudged it.

But anyway I thought you would like a picture of the INSIDE of my
new big house for a change. This is the chief hall under the largest dome,
where we pile the presents usually ready to load on the sleighs at the doors.
PB & I built it nearly all ourselves, and laid all the blue and mauve tiles.
The banisters and roof are not quite straight, but it does'nt really matter.
I painted the pictures on the walls of the trees and stars and suns and
moons. Then I said to PB "I shall leave the freeze to you". He said
'I should have thought there was enough freeze outside — and your
colours inside: all purply-greyzy-bluey-palegreeny are cold enough too'
I said "dont be a silly bear: do your best, there's a good old polar" — and
look at the result!! Icicles all round the hall to make a freeze (he
can't spell very well), and starful bright colour to make a warm freeze!!

Well my dears I hope you will like the things I am bringing: nearly all you
asked for and lots of other little things you didnt & which I thought of
at the last minute. I hope you will share the railway things and farm
and animals often, and not think they are absolutely only for the one whose
stocking they were in. Take care of them for they are some of my very
best things. Love to Chris: love to Michael: love to John who
must be getting very big as he does'nt write to me any more (so I simply
had to guess paints — I hope they were all right: PB chose them: he says
he knows what John likes because J. likes bears)

Your loving ✶ ✶ ✶

FATHER CHRISTMAS

NOT MY
FAULT
P.C. DID
BANISTERS

AND
MY LOVE
PB

the hall to make a freeze (F. R. E. E. Z. E.) (he can't spell very well), and fearful bright colour to make a warm freeze!!!

Well, my dears, I hope you will like the things I am bringing: nearly all you asked for and lots of other little things you didn't, and which I thought of at the last minute. I hope you will share the railway things and farm and animals often, and not think they are absolutely only for the one whose stocking they were in. Take care of them, for they are some of my very best things.

Love to Chris: love to Michael: love to John who must be getting very big as he doesn't write to me any more (so I simply had to guess paints – I hope they were all right: Polar Bear chose them; he says he knows what John likes because John likes bears).

Your loving Father Christmas

And my love, Polar Bear

BOXING DAY
1928

I am frightfully
sorry — I gave
this to the P.B. to
post and he forgot
all about it! We
found it on the hall
table to-day.

But you must forgive
him: he has worked
very hard for me & is
dreadfully tired. We
have had a busy Christ-
mas. Very windy here:
It blew several sleighs
over before they could
start—

Love again

FC X

Boxing Day, 1928

I am frightfully sorry – I gave this to the Polar Bear
to post and he forgot all about it! We found it on the
hall table – today.

But you must forgive him: he has worked very hard
for me and is dreadfully tired. We have had a busy
Christmas. Very windy here. It blew several sleighs
over before they could start.

Love again, Father Christmas

1929

November 1929

Dear boys,

My paw is better. I was cutting Christmas trees when I hurt it. Don't you think my writing is much better too? Father Christmas is very bisy already. So am I. We have had hevy snow and sum of our messengers got buerried and sum lost: that is whi you have not herd lately.

Love to John for his birthday. Father Christmas says my English spelling is not good. I kant help it. We don't speak English here, only Arktik (which you don't know. We also make our letters different – I have made mine like Arktik letters for you to see. We always rite ↑ for T and V for U. This is sum Arktik langwidge wich means "Goodby till I see you next and I hope it will bee soon." – Mára mesta an ni véla tye ento, ya rato nea.

P. B.

My real name is Karhu but I don't tell most peeple.

P.S. I like letters and think Cristofers are nice

DEAR BOYS

NOV 1920

    MY PAW IS BETTER. I WAS CUTTING CHRISTMAS
TREES WEN I HURT IT. DONT YOU THINK MY WRITING
IS MUCH BETTER TOO? FATHER X IS VERY BISY
ALREADY, SO AM I. WE HAVE HAD HEVY SNOW, AND
SUM OF OUR MESSENGERS GOT BVERRIED AND SUM
LOST: THAT IS WHI YOU HAVE NOT HERD LATELY.
LOVE TO JOHN FOR HIS BIRTHDAY. FATHER X SAYS
MI ENGLISH SPELLING IS NOT GOOD. I KANT HELP IT. WE
DONT SPEAK ENGLISH HERE, ONLY ARKTIK (WHICH YOU

DONT KNOW. WE ALSO MAKE OUR LETTERS DIFFERENT
~~~ I HAVE MADE MINE LIKE ARKTIK LETTERS FOR YOU TO
SEE. WE ALWAYS RITE ↑ FOR T AND V FOR U.
THIS IS SUM ARKTIK LANGWIDGE WICH MEANS
"GOOD BY TILL I SEE YOU NEXT AND I HOPE IT
WILL BEE SOON." ~~~ MARA MESTA AN NI VELA TYE
ENTO YA RATO NEA

P. B.

MY REAL NAME IS **KARHU** BUT I DON'T TELL
MOST PEEPLE.

MI PAW

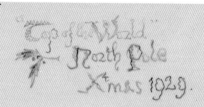

"Top of the World"
North Pole
X'mas 1929.

Dear Boys & Girls

It is alight Christmas again I am glad to say—
the Northern Lights have been specially good.

There is a lot to tell you. You have heard
that the Great Polar Bear chopped his paw when he
was cutting Christmas Trees. His right
one— I mean not his left, of course. He
was wrong to cut it —a pity too for he spent
a lot of the Summer learning to write
better so as to help me with my winter letters.

We had a Bonfire this year (to please the
P.B.) to celebrate the coming in of winter.
The Snow-elves let off all the
rockets together which surprised us both. I have
tried to draw you a picture of it but really there
were hundreds of rockets. You can't see
the elves at all against the snow background.
The Bonfire made a hole in the ice & woke
up the Great Seal who happened to be underneath. The P.B. let off 20000 silver

48

Top of the World,
North Pole
Xmas 1929

Dear Boys and Girl

It is a light Christmas again, I am glad to say – the
Northern Lights have been specially good. There is
a lot to tell you. You have heard that the Great Polar

Bear chopped his paw when he was cutting Christmas Trees. His right one – I mean not his left; of course it was wrong to cut it, and a pity too for he spent a lot of the Summer learning to write better so as to help me with my winter letters.

We had a Bonfire this year (to please the Polar Bear) to celebrate the coming in of winter. The Snow-elves let off all the rockets together, which surprised us both. I have tried to draw you a picture of it, but really there were hundreds of rockets. You can't see the elves at all against the snow background.

The Bonfire made a hole in the ice and woke up the Great Seal, who happened to be underneath. The Polar Bear let off 20,000 silver sparklers afterwards – used up all my stock, so that is why I had none to send you. Then he went for a holiday!!! – to north Norway, and stayed with a wood-cutter called Olaf, and came back with paw all bandaged just at the beginning of our busy times.

There seem more children than ever in England, Norway, Denmark, Sweden, and Germany, which are the countries I specially look after (and of course North America and Canada) – not to speak of getting stuff down to the South Pole for children who expect to be looked after though they have gone to live in New Zealand or Australia or South Africa or China.

sparklers afterwards—used up all my stock, so that is why I had none to send you.

Then he went for a holiday!!! — to north Norway & stayed with a wood-cutter called Olaf & came back with his paw all bandaged just at the beginning of our busy times. There seem more children than ever in England, Norway, Denmark, Sweden, & Germany, which are the countries I specially look after (& ofcourse North America & Canada)—not to speak of sending stuff down to the South Pole for children who expect to be looked after though they have gone to live in New Zealand or Australia or South Africa or China. It is a good thing clocks don't tell the same time all over the world or I should never get round, although when my magic is strongest —at Xmas — I can do about a thousand stockings a minute, if I have it all planned out beforehand. You could hardly guess the enormous piles of lists I make out — I seldom get them mixed. But I am rather worried this year. You can guess from my pictures what happened. The first one shews you my office & stocking-room, and the P.B. reading out names while I copy them down. We had awful gales here, worse than you did, tearing clouds of snow to a million tatters, screaming like demons, burying my house almost up to the roofs.

52

It is a good thing clocks don't tell the same time all over the world or I should never get round, although when my magic is strongest – at Christmas – I can do about a thousand stockings a minute, if I have it all planned out beforehand. You could hardly guess the enormous piles of lists I make out. I seldom get them mixed.

But I am rather worried this year. In my office and packing-room, the Polar Bear reads out names while I copy them down. We had awful gales here, worse than you did, tearing clouds of snow to a million tatters, screaming like demons, burying my house almost up to the roofs. Just at the worst, the Polar Bear said it was stuffy! and opened a north window before I could stop him. You can guess the result – the North Polar Bear was buried in papers and lists; but that did not stop him laughing.

Also all my red and green ink was upset, as well as black, – so I am writing in chalk and pencil. I have some black ink left, and the Polar Bear is using it to address parcels.

I liked all your letters – very much indeed my dears. Nobody, or very few, write so much or so nicely to me. I'm specially pleased with Christopher's card, and his letters, and with his learning to write, so I am sending him a fountain pen and also a special picture for himself. It shows me crossing the sea on the upper

North wind, while a South West gale – reindeer hate
it – is raising big waves below.

This must be all now. I send you all my love. One
more stocking to fill this year! I hope you will like
your new house and the things I bring you.

Your Old Father Christmas

Just at the worst the PB said it was stuffy, & opened a north window before I could stop him. Look at the result — only I actually the NPB was barred in papers & lists; but that did not stop him laughing. Also all my red & green ink was upset, as well as black — so I am writing in chalk & pencil. I have some black ink left (but I know you like colours) & the PB is using it to address parcels.

I liked all your letters — very much indeed my dears. Nobody, or very few, write so much or so nicely to me. I am specially pleased with Xtopher's card, and his letters, and with his learning to write. So I am sending him a FOUNTAIN PEN & also a special picture for himself. It shows me crossing the sea on the upper NORTH wind, while a SOUTH WEST gale — reindeer hate it — is raising big waves below.

This must be all now. I send you all my love. One more stocking to fill this year! I hope you will like your new house & the things I bring you.

Your old

Fr. Xmas

Nov 28th 1930.

Fr Christmas has got all your
letters! What a lot, especially
from C & M! Thank you, and
also Reddy and your bears, & other
animals.

I am just beginning to get awfully busy. Let
me know more about what you specially want.
Also (if you can find out) what anyone else likes
Por Mummy or Auntie (I mean C & Miss) Grove
wants. P.B sends love. He is just getting better.
He has had whooping Cough !! F.N.C.

J & M & C Tolkien

By messenger

56

1930

November 28th 1930

Father Christmas has got all your letters! What a lot, especially from Christopher and Michael! Thank you, and also Reddy and your bears, and other animals.

I am just beginning to get awfully busy. Let me know more about what you specially want.

Polar Bear sends love. He is just getting better. He has had Whooping Cough!!

Father Nicholas Christmas

Top of the World,
North Pole
Christmas 1930
Not finished until Christmas Eve, 24th December

My dears,

I have enjoyed all your letters. I am dreadfully sorry
there has been no time to answer them, and even now
I have not time to finish my picture for you properly
or to send you a full long letter like I mean to.

I hope you will like your stockings this year: I tried
to find what you asked for, but the stores have been
in rather a muddle – you see the Polar Bear has been
ill. He had whooping cough first of all. I could not let
him help with the packing and sorting which begins
in November – because it would be simply awful if
any of my children caught Polar whooping cough
and barked like bears on Boxing Day. So I had to do
everything myself in the preparations.

Of course, Polar Bear has done his best – he cleaned
up and mended my sleigh, and looked after the
reindeer while I was busy. That is how the really bad

Top of the World
N°
Christmas 1930
December 23rd !! Not finished until Christmas Eve. 24th

My dears,

   I have enjoyed all your letters & I am dreadfully sorry there has been no time to answer them & even now I haven't time to finish my picture for you properly or to send you a full long letter like I meant to.

   I hope you will like your stockings this year: I tried to find what you asked for, but the stores I have been in are rather a muddle — you can see the Polar Bear has been ill. He had whooping cough first of all (!) I could not let him help with the packing & sorting which begins in November — because it would be simply awful if any of my children caught Polar Whooping cough & barked like bears on Boxing-Day. So I had to do everything myself in the preparations. Of course P.B. has done his best — he cleaned & mended my sleigh and looked after the reindeer while I was busy. That is how the really bad accident happened. Early this month we had a most awful snowstorm (nearly 2 feet of snow) followed by an awful fog. The poor P.B. went out to the Reindeer-stables, & got lost and nearly buried: I did not miss him or go to look for him for a long while. His chest hadn't got well from Wh. Cough & this made him frightfully ill & he was in bed until three days ago. Everything has gone wrong, & there has been no one to look after my messengers properly.

   Aren't you glad the P.B. is better? We had a party of Snow-boys (sons of the Snow-men which are the only sort of people that live near — not of course men made of snow, though my gardener who is the oldest of all the snowmen sometimes draws a picture of a made snow-man instead of writing his name) and Polar-Cubs (the P.B.'s nephews) on Saturday as soon as he felt well enough. He didn't eat much tea, but when the big cracker went off & he knew away his cap, and leaped in the air and has been well ever since.

1930

Party of Snowboys & Polar-cubs to celebrate P.B's recovery.

P.B recovers!

accident happened. Early this month we had a most awful snowstorm (nearly six feet of snow) followed by an awful fog. The poor Polar Bear went out to the reindeer-stables, and got lost and nearly buried: I did not miss him or go to look for him for a long while. His chest had not got well from whooping cough so this made him frightfully ill, and he was in bed until three days ago. Everything has gone wrong, and there has been no one to look after my messengers properly.

Aren't you glad the Polar Bear is better? We had a party of Snowboys (sons of the Snowmen, which are the only sort of people that live near – not of course men made of snow, though my gardener who is the oldest of all the snowmen sometimes draws a picture of a made Snowman instead of writing his name) and Polar Cubs (the Polar Bear's nephews) on Saturday as soon as he felt well enough.

He didn't eat much tea, but when the big cracker went off after, he threw away his rug, and leaped in the air and has been well ever since.

I've drawn you pictures of everything that happened – Polar Bear telling a story after all the things had been cleared away; me finding Polar Bear in the snow, and Polar Bear sitting with his feet in hot mustard and water to stop him shivering. It didn't – and he sneezed so terribly he blew five candles out.

The top picture shows F.C. telling a story after all the things had been cleared away. The little pictures show me finding F.C.B. in the snow, & F.C.B. sitting with his feet in hot mustard & water to stop him shivering. It isn't — if he sneezed so terribly he blew five candles out. Still he is all right now — I know because he has been at his tricks again — quarrelling with the Snowman (my gardener) & pushing him through the roof of his snow house; & packing lumps of ice instead of presents in naughty children's parcels. That might be a good idea only he never told me & some of them (with ice) were put in warm storerooms & melted all over good children's presents!

Well my dears there is lots more I should like to say — about my green brother and my father old Grandfather Yule and why we were left called Nicholas after the Saint (whose day is December sixth) who used to give secret presents, sometimes throwing purses of money through the window. But I must hurry away — I am late already & I am afraid you may not get this in time.

Kisses to You all ✳ Fr. N. Christmas.

P.S.

{ Chris. has no need to be frightened of me. }

Still he is all right now – I know because he has been at his tricks again: quarrelling with the Snowman (my gardener) and pushing him through the roof of his snow house; and packing lumps of ice instead of presents in naughty children's parcels. That might be a good idea, only he never told me and some of them (with ice) were put in warm storerooms and melted all over good children's presents!

Well my dears there is lots more I should like to say – about my green brother and my father, old Grandfather Yule, and why we were both called Nicholas after the Saint (whose day is December sixth) who used to give secret presents, sometimes throwing purses of money through the window. But I must hurry away – I am late already and I am afraid you may not get this in time.

Kisses to you all,

Father Nicholas Christmas

P.S. (Chris has no need to be frightened of me).

Cliff house
Oct. 31
1931

Dear Children,
        Already I have got
some letters   from you!
You are getting busy early. I
have not begun to think about
Christmas yet. It has been very
warm in the North this year, &
there has been very little snow so
far. We are just getting in
our Xmas fire = wood.

        This is just to say my messengers
will be coming round regularly now

1931

Cliff House
October 31st 1931

Dear Children,

Already I have got some letters from you! You are
getting busy early. I have not begun to think about
Christmas yet. It has been very warm in the North this
year, and there has been very little snow so far. We
are just getting in our Christmas firewood.

This is just to say my messengers will be coming
round regularly now Winter has begun – we shall be
having a bonfire tomorrow – and I shall like to hear
from you: Sunday and Wednesday evenings are the
best times to post to me.

The Polar Bear is quite well and fairly good – (though
you never know what he will do when the Christmas
rush begins.) Send my love to John.

Your loving
Father Nicholas Christmas

Winter has begun —— We shall be having a bonfire tomorrow —— & I shall like to hear from you: Sunday & Wednesday evenings are the best times to post to me.

The P.B. is quite well & fairly good —— though you never know what he will do when the Xmas rush begins. Send my love to John.

Yr loving

Fr Xmas

GLAD FR X HAS WAKT VP. HE SLEPT
NEARLY ALL THIS HOT SVMMER. I
WISH WE KOOD HAVE SNOW. MY
COAT IS QVITE YELLOW. LOVE PB

Glad Father Christmas has wakt up. He slept nearly all this hot summer. I wish we kood have snow. My coat is quite yellow.

Love Polar Bear

Cliff House,
North Pole
December 23rd 1931

My dear Children

I hope you will like the little things I have sent you.
You seem to be most interested in Railways just now,
so I am sending you mostly things of that sort. I send
as much love as ever, in fact more. We have both, the

My latest portrait. — Father Christmas packing 1931. I gve to you all. Your loving F^r N.C.

old Polar Bear and I, enjoyed having so many nice letters from you and your pets. If you think we have not read them you are wrong; but if you find that not many of the things you asked for have come, and not perhaps quite as many as sometimes, remember that this Christmas all over the world there are a terrible number of poor and starving people.

Cliff House
North Pole
December 23rd 1931

My dear Children,

I hope you will like the little things I have sent you. You seem to be most interested in Railways just now, so I am sending you mostly things of that sort. I send as much love as ever, in fact more. We have both the old P.B. and I enjoyed having so many nice letters from you and your pets. If you think we have not read them you are wrong; but if you find that not many of the things you asked for have come, I hope not, perhaps quite as many as sometimes remember that this Christmas all over the world there are a terrible number of poor & starving people. I & also my Green Brother have had to do some collecting of food & clothes, and toys too, for the children whose fathers & mothers and friends cannot give them anything, sometimes not even dinner. I know yours won't forget you. So, my dears, I hope you will be happy this Xmas & not quarrel & will have some good games with your Railway all together. Don't forget old Father Christmas when you light your tree.*

It has gone on being warm up here as I told you — not what you would call warm, but warm for the N.P. — with very little snow. The N.P.B., if you know who I mean, has been lazy & sleepy as a result, & very slow over packing, or any job except eating — he has enjoyed sampling and tasting the food parcels this year (to see if they were fresh & good, he said). But that is not the worst — I should hardly feel it was Christmas if he didn't do something ridiculous. You will never guess what he did this time! I sent him down into one of my cellars — the Cracker-hole we call it, where I keep thousands of boxes of crackers (you would like to see them, rows upon rows all with their lids off to show the kinds & colours) — well, I wanted 20 boxes, & was busy sorting soldiers & farm things,

‡ SOMEBODY HAZ TO — AND I FOUND STONES IN SOME OF THE KURRANTS

69

So I sent him; and he was so lazy he took two Snow-boys (who aren't allowed down there) to help him. They started pulling crackers out of boxes, and he tried to box them (the boys' ears I mean), and they dodged and he fell over & let his candle fall—bang-poof! into my fire-work crackers & boxes of sparklers. I could hear the noise, & smell the smell in the hall, & when I rushed down I saw nothing but smoke and fizzing stars, & old PB was rolling over on the floor with sparks sizzling in his coat: he has quite a bare patch burnt on his back.*⊙ The Snow-boys roared with laughter & then ran away. They said it was a splendid sight, but they won't come to my party on St Stephen's Day; they have had more than their share already.

Two of the PB's nephews have been staying here for some time— Paksu and Valkotukka ("fat" and "white-hair" they say it means). They are fat-tummied polar-cubs, & are very funny boxing one another & rolling about. But another time, I shall have them on Boxing-day & not just at packing-time. I fell over them fourteen times a day last week. And Valkotukka swallowed a ball of red string thinking it was cake and he got it all wound up inside and had a tangled cough—he couldn't sleep at night, but, I thought it rather served him right for eating holly in my bed. It was the same cub that poured all the black ink yesterday into the fire—to make night: it did, & a very smelly smoky one. We lost Paksu all last Wednesday & found him on Thursday morning asleep in a cupboard in the kitchen; he had eaten two whole pudd-ings raw. They seem to be growing up just like their uncle!

Goodbye now. I shall soon be off on my travels once more. You need not believe any pictures you see of me in aeroplanes or motors. I cannot drive one, & I don't want to; and they are too slow anyway (not to mention smell), they cannot compare with my own reindeer, which I train myself. They are all very I-well this year & I expect my posts will be in very good time. I have got some new young ones this Christ-mas from Lapland (a great place for wizards) but these are WHIZZERS! One day I will send you a picture of my deer-stables and harness-houses. I am expecting that John, although he is now over 14, will hang up his stock-ing this last time; but I don't forget people even when they are past stocking-age, not until they forget me. So I send LOVE to you ALL, & especially little PM, who is beginning her stocking-days & I hope they will be happy.

Your loving Father Christmas

I (and also my Green Brother) have had to do some collecting of food and clothes, and toys too, for the children whose fathers and mothers and friends cannot give them anything, sometimes not even dinner. I know yours won't forget you.

So, my dears, I hope you will be happy this Christmas and not quarrel, and will have some good games with your Railway all together. Don't forget old Father Christmas, when you light your tree.

Nor me!

It has gone on being warm up here as I told you – not what you would call warm, but warm for the North Pole, with very little snow. The North Polar Bear, if you know who I mean, has been lazy and sleepy as a result, and very slow over packing, or any job except eating. He has enjoyed sampling and tasting the food parcels this year (to see if they were fresh and good, he said).

Somebody haz to – and I found stones in some of the kurrants.

But that is not the worst – I should hardly feel it was Christmas if he didn't do something ridiculous. You will never guess what he did this time! I sent him down into one of my cellars – the Cracker-hole we call it – where I keep thousands of boxes of crackers (you would like to see them, rows upon rows, all with their lids off to show the kinds of colours).

Well, I wanted 20 boxes, and was busy sorting soldiers and farm things, so I sent him; and he was so lazy he took two Snowboys (who aren't allowed down there) to help him. They started pulling crackers out of boxes, and he tried to box them (the boys' ears I mean), and they dodged and he fell over, and let his candle fall right POOF! into my firework crackers and boxes of sparklers.

I could hear the noise, and smell the smell in the hall; and when I rushed down I saw nothing but smoke and fizzing stars, and old Polar Bear was rolling over on the floor with sparks sizzling in his coat: he has quite a bare patch burnt on his back.

It looked fine!
That's where Father Christmas spilled the gravy on my back at dinner!

The Snowboys roared with laughter and then ran away. They said it was a splendid sight – but they won't come to my party on St Stephen's Day; they have had more than their share already.

Two of the Polar Bear's nephews have been staying here for some time – Paksu and Valkotukka ('fat' and 'white-hair' they say it means). They are fat-tummied polar-cubs, and are very funny boxing one another and rolling about. But another time, I shall have them on Boxing Day, and not just at packing-time. I fell over them fourteen times a day last week.

1931 -32

N.P.B.   KARHU

LOVE FROM KARHU, PAKSU, AND VALKOTUKKA.   V

This is all drawn by N.P.B. Don't you think he is getting better. But the green ink is mine — & he didn't ask for it.

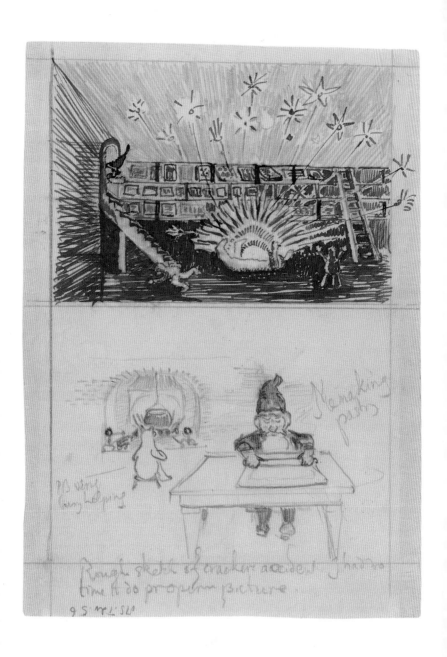

Nanaking party

NB very funny helping

Rough sketch of cracker accident. I had no time to do proper picture.

175.74.56

And Valkotukka swallowed a ball of red string, thinking it was cake, and he got it all wound up inside and had a tangled cough – he couldn't sleep at night, but I thought it rather served him right for putting holly in my bed.

It was the same cub that poured all the black ink yesterday into the fire – to make night: it did and a very smelly smoky one. We lost Paksu all last Wednesday and found him on Thursday morning asleep in a cupboard in the kitchen; he had eaten two whole puddings raw. They seem to be growing up just like their uncle.

Not fair!

Goodbye now. I shall soon be off on my travels once more. You need not believe any pictures you see of me in aeroplanes or motors. I cannot drive one, and don't want to; and they are too slow anyway (not to mention smell). They cannot compare with my own reindeer, which I train myself. They are all very well this year, and I expect my posts will be in very good time. I have got some new young ones this Christmas from Lapland (a great place for wizards; but these are WHIZZERS).

Bad!

One day I will send you a picture of my deer-stables and harness-houses. I am expecting that John, although he is now over 14, will hang up his stocking this last time; but I don't forget people even when they are past stocking-age, not until they forget me. So I send LOVE to you ALL, and especially little PM, who is beginning her stocking-days and I hope they will be happy.

Your loving Father Christmas

P.S. This is all drawn by North Polar Bear. Don't you think he is getting better? But the green ink is mine – and he didn't ask for it.

1932

Cliff House,
North Pole.
November 30th 1932

My dear children

Thank you for your nice letters. I have not forgotten
you. I am very late this year and very worried – a
very funny thing has happened. The Polar Bear has

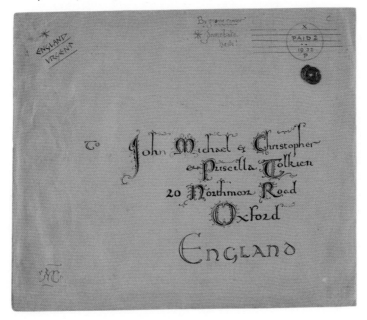

To John, Michael & Christopher
and Priscilla Tolkien
20 Northmoor Road
Oxford
England

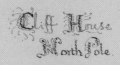

Cliff House
North Pole.

November 30th
1932.

My Dear Children,

Thank you for your nice letters I have
not forgotten you. I am very late this year & very
worried—a very funny thing has happened. The
P.B. has disappeared, & I don't know where he
is. I have not seen him since the beginning of this
month, & I am getting anxious. Tomorrow December, the Christmas month, begins, & I don't
know what I shall do without him.

I am glad you are all well & your many
pets. The snowbabies holidays begin tomorrow.
I wish P.B. was here to look after them. Love
to M.C. & P. Please send P. my love when you
write to him.
Father ☧ Christmas.

78

disappeared, and I don't know where he is. I have not seen him since the beginning of this month, and I am getting anxious. Tomorrow December, the Christmas month, begins, and I don't know what I shall do without him.

I am glad you are all well and your many pets. The Snowbabies holidays begin tomorrow. I wish Polar Bear was here to look after them. Love to Michael, Christopher and Priscilla. Please send John my love when you write to him.

Father N. Christmas.

Cliff House
near the North Pole
December 23rd.
1932.

My dear children,

There is a lot to tell you. First of all a Merry Christmas! But there have been lots of adventures you will want to hear about. It all began with the funny noises underground which started in the summer & got worse & worse. I was afraid an earthquake might happen. The N.P.B. says he suspected what was wrong from the beginning. I only wish he had said something to me; & anyway it can't be quite true, as he was fast asleep when it began & did not wake up till about Michael's birthday. However, he went off for a walk one day, at the end of November I think, & never came back! About a fortnight ago I began to be really worried, for after all the dear old thing is really a lot of help, inspite of accidents, & very amusing. One Friday evening (Dec. 9th) there was a bumping at the front door & a snuffling. I thought he had come back, & lost his key (as often before); but when I opened the door there was another very old bear there, a very fat & funny-shaped one. Actually it was the eldest of the few remaining cave-bears, old Mr Cave-Brown-Cave himself (I had not seen him for centuries).

"Do you want your North Polar Bear?" he said. "If you do you had better come & get him!"

It turned out he was lost in the caves (belonging to Mr CBC or so he said) not far from the ruins of my old house. He says he found a hole in the side of a hill & went inside because it was snowing. He slipped down a long slope, & lots of rock fell after him, & he found he could not climb up or get out again. But almost at once he smelt goblin! & became interested & started to explore. Not very wise; for of course goblins can't hurt him, but their caves are very dangerous. Naturally he soon got quite lost, & the goblins shut off all their lights, & made queer noises & false echoes.

Goblins are to us very much what rats are to you, only worse because they are very clever, & only better because there are in these parts very few. We thought there were none left. Long ago we had great trouble with them, that was about 1453 I believe, but we got the help of the Gnomes, who are their greatest enemies, & cleared them out. Anyway there was poor old P.B. lost in the dark all among them, & all alone until he met Mr CBC (who lives there). CBC can see pretty well in the dark, & he offered to take P.B. to his private back-door. So they set off together; but the goblins were very excited & angry (P.B. had boxed one or two flat that came and poked him in the dark), & had said

Cliff House,
near the North Pole
December 23rd 1932

My dear children,

There is a lot to tell you. First of all a Merry Christmas!
But there have been lots of adventures you will want
to hear about. It all began with the funny noises
underground which started in the summer and got
worse and worse. I was afraid an earthquake might
happen. The North Polar Bear says he suspected what
was wrong from the beginning. I only wish he had said
something to me; and anyway it can't be quite true,
as he was fast asleep when it began, and did not wake
up till about Michael's birthday.

However, he went off for a walk one day, at the end
of November I think, and never came back! About a
fortnight ago I began to be really worried, for after
all the dear old thing is really a lot of help, in spite of
accidents, and very amusing.

One Friday evening (December 9th) there was a
bumping at the front door, and a snuffling. I thought

he had come back, and lost his key (as often before); but when I opened the door there was another very old bear there, a very fat and funny-shaped one. Actually it was the eldest of the few remaining cave-bears, old Mr Cave Bear himself (I had not seen him for centuries).

"Do you want your North Polar Bear?" he said. "If you do you had better come and get him!" It turned out he was lost in the caves (belonging to Mr Cave Bear, or so he says) not far from the ruins of my old house. He says he found a hole in the side of a hill and went inside because it was snowing. He slipped down a long slope, and lots of rock fell after him, and he found he could not climb up or get out again.

But almost at once he smelt goblin! and became interested, and started to explore. Not very wise; for of course goblins can't hurt him, but their caves are very dangerous.

Naturally he soon got quite lost, and the goblins shut off all their lights, and made queer noises and false echoes.

Goblins are to us very much what rats are to you, only worse because they are very clever; and only better because there are, in these parts, very few. We thought there were none left. Long ago we had great trouble with them – that was about 1453 I believe – but we got the help of the Gnomes, who are their greatest enemies, and cleared them out.

some very nasty things to them all), and they enticed away by imitating CBC's voice, which of course they know very well. So PB got into a frightful dark part all full of different passages, & he lost CBC & CBC lost him.

'Light is what we need' said CBC to me. So I got some of my special sparkling torches — which I sometimes use in my deepest cellars — & we set off that night. The caves are wonderful. I knew they were there, but not how many or how big they were. Of course the goblins went off into the deepest holes & corners, & we soon found PB. He was getting quite long & thin with hunger, as he had been in the caves about a fortnight. He said ' I should soon have been able to squeeze through a goblin-crack'.

PB himself was astonished when I brought light; for the most remarkable thing is that the walls of these caves are all covered with pictures, cut into the rock or painted on in red and brown and black. Some of them are very good (mostly of animals), & some are queer & some bad, & there are many strange marks, signs & scribbles, some of which have a nasty look & I am sure have something to do with black magic. CBC says these caves belong to him & have belonged to him or his family since the days of his great-great-great-great-great-great-great-great-great-(multiplied by ten) grandfather; and the bears first had the idea of decorating the walls & used to scratch pictures on them at soft parts — it was useful for sharpening the claws. Then MEN came along — imagine it! CBC says there were lots about at one time, long ago, then the North Pole was somewhere else. That was long before my time & I have never heard Gt Grandfather Yule mention it, even. So I don't know if he is talking nonsense or not). Many of the pictures were done by these cave-men — the best ones, especially the bigones (almost life-size) of animals, some of which have since disappeared: there are dragons and quite a lot of mammoths. Men also put some of the black marks & pictures there; but the goblins have scribbled all over the place. They can't draw well & any way they like nasty queer shapes best. NPB got quite excited when he saw all these things.

He said: These cave-people could draw better than you, daddy Noel; and wouldn't your young friends just like to see some really good pictures (especially some properly drawn bears) for a change!'

Rather rude, I thought; only a joke, as I take a lot of trouble over my Christmas pictures: some of them take quite a minute to do, & though I only send them to special friends, I have a good many in different places. So just to show him (& to please you) I have copied a whole page from the wall of the chief central cave, & send you a copy. It is not perhaps quite as well drawn as the originals, (which are very very much larger) — except the goblin parts, which are easy. They are the only parts the PB can do at all. He says he likes them best, but that is only because he can copy them.

Anyway, there was poor old Polar Bear lost in the dark all among them, and all alone until he met Mr Cave Bear (who lives there). Cave Bear can see pretty well in the dark, and he offered to take Polar Bear to his private back-door.

So they set off together, but the goblins were very excited and angry (Polar Bear had boxed one or two flat that came and poked him in the dark, and had said some very nasty things to them all); and they enticed him away by imitating Cave Bear's voice, which of course they know very well. So Polar Bear got into a frightful dark part, all full of different passages, and he lost Cave Bear, and Cave Bear lost him.

"Light is what we need." said Cave Bear to me. So I got some of my special sparkling torches – which I sometimes use in my deepest cellars – and we set off that night.

The caves are wonderful. I knew they were there, but not how many or how big they were. Of course the goblins went off into the deepest holes and corners, and we soon found Polar Bear. He was getting quite long and thin with hunger, as he had been in the caves about a fortnight. He said, "I should soon have been able to squeeze through a goblin-crack."

Polar Bear himself was astonished when I brought light; for the most remarkable thing is that the walls of these caves are all covered with pictures, cut into the rock or painted on in red and brown and black.

Some of them are very good (mostly of animals), and some are queer and some bad; and there are many strange marks, signs and scribbles, some of which have a nasty look, and I am sure have something to do with black magic.

Cave Bear says these caves belong to him, and have belonged to him or his family since the days of his great-great-great-great-great-great-great-great-great (multiplied by ten) grandfather; and the bears first had the idea of decorating the walls, and used to scratch pictures on them on soft parts – it was useful for sharpening the claws.

Then Men came along – imagine it! Cave Bear says there were lots about at one time, long ago, when the North Pole was somewhere else. (That was long before my time, and I have never heard old Grandfather Yule mention it even, so I don't know if he is talking nonsense or not).

Many of the pictures were done by these cave-men – the best ones, especially the big ones (almost life-size) of animals, some of which have since disappeared: there are dragons and quite a lot of mammoths. Men also put some of the black marks and pictures there; but the goblins have scribbled all over the place. They can't draw well and anyway they like nasty queer shapes best.

At the bottom of the page you will see a whole row of goblin pictures — they must be very old, because the goblin fighters are sitting on drasils: a very queer sort of dwarf 'dachshund' horse creature, they used to use, but they have died out long ago. I believe the Red Gnomes finished them off, somewhere about Edward the Fourth's time. You will see some more on the pillar in my picture of the Caves.

Doesn't the hairy rhinoceros look wicked; there is also a nasty look in the mammoth's eyes. You will also see an ox, a stag, a bear, & cave-bear (portrait of Mr. C.B.C.'s seventy first ancestor, he says) and some other kind of polar-ish but not quite polar bear. NPB would like to believe it is a portrait of one of his ancestors! Just under the bears you can see what is the best a goblin can do at drawing reindeer. !!!

You have been so good in writing to me (& such beautiful letters too), that I have tried to draw you some specially nice pictures this year. At the top of my 'Christmas card' is a picture, imaginary, but more or less as it really is, of me arriving over Oxford. Your house is just about where the three little black points stick up out of the shadows at the right. I am coming from the north and see — & note NOT with 12 pair of deer as you will see in some books. I usually use 7 pair (14 is such a nice number), & at Christmas, especially if I am hurried, I add my 2 special white ones in front.

Next comes a picture of me and CBC & NPB exploring the Caves — I will tell you more about that in a minute. The last picture is also imaginary, that is it hasn't happened yet. It soon will. On St. Stephen's Day, when all the rush is over, I am going to have a rowdy party: the CBC's grandchildren (they are exactly like live teddy-bears), snow-babies, some children of the Red Gnomes, & of course polar cubs, including Paksu & Valkotukka, will be there. Don't you like my new green trousers? They were a present from my green brother, but I only wear them at home. Goblins any way dislike green, so I found them useful. You see, when I rescued PB, who hadn't finished the Adventures. At the beginning of this week we went into the cellars to get up the stuff for England.

I said to PB 'Somebody has been disarranging things here!' 'Paksu & V.' I expect, he said. But it wasn't.

Next day things were much worse, especially among the railway-things, lots of which seemed to be missing. I ought to have guessed, & P & amway ought to have mentioned his guess to me. Last Saturday we went down & found nearly every thing had disapp-ared out of the main cellar! Imagine my state of mind! Nothing hardly to send to anybody & too little time to get or make enough new stuff. NPB said 'I smell goblin string.' Of course: it was obvious — they love mechanical toys (though they quickly smash them & want more & more & more); & practically all the Hornby things had gone! Eventually we found a large hole (but not big enough for us) leading to a tunnel behind

North Polar Bear got quite excited when he saw all these things. He said: "These cave-people could draw better than you, Daddy Noel; and wouldn't your young friends just like to see some really good pictures (especially some properly drawn bears) for a change!"

Rather rude, I thought, if only a joke; as I take a lot of trouble over my Christmas pictures: some of them take quite a minute to do; and though I only send them to special friends, I have a good many in different places. So just to show him (and to please you) I have copied a whole page from the wall of the chief central cave, and I send you a copy.

It is not, perhaps, quite as well drawn as the originals (which are very, very much larger) – except the goblin parts, which are easy. They are the only parts the Polar Bear can do at all. He says he likes them best, but that is only because he can copy them.

The goblin pictures must be very old, because the goblin fighters are sitting on drasils: a very queer sort of dwarf 'dachshund' horse creature they used to use, but they have died out long ago. I believe the Red Gnomes finished them off, somewhere about Edward the Fourth's time.

The animal drawings are magnificent. The hairy rhinoceros looks wicked. There is also a nasty look in the mammoth's eyes. Also the ox, stag, boar, and cave-bear (portrait of Mr Cave Bear's seventy-first ancestor, he says), and some other kind of polarish but not quite polar bear. North Polar Bear would like to believe it is a portrait of one of his ancestors! Just under the bears is the best a goblin can do at drawing reindeer!!!

You have been so good in writing to me (and such beautiful letters too), that I have tried to draw you some specially nice pictures this year. At the top of my 'Christmas card' is a picture, imaginary, but more or less as it really is, of me arriving over Oxford. Your house is just about where the three little black points stick up out of the shadows at the right. I am coming from the north, and note, NOT with 12 pair of deer, as you will see in some books. I usually use 7 pair (14 is such a nice number), and at Christmas, especially if I am hurried, I add my 2 special white ones in front.

Next comes a picture of me and Cave Bear and North Polar Bear exploring the Caves – I will tell you more about that in a minute. The last picture hasn't happened yet. It soon will. On St Stephen's Day, when all the rush is over, I am going to have a rowdy party: the Cave Bear's grandchildren (they are exactly like live teddy-bears), Snowbabies, some children of the Red Gnomes, and of course Polar Cubs, including Paksu and Valkotukka, will be there.

I'm wearing a pair of new green trousers. They were a present from my green brother, but I only wear them

some packing-cases in the West-Cellar. As you will expect we rushed off
to find CBC, & we went back to the caves. We soon understood the
queer noises. It was plain the goblins long ago had burrowed a tunnel from
the caves to my old home (which was not so far from the end of their hills), &
had stolen a good many things. We found some things more than a hundred
years old even a few parcels still addressed to your great-grand-people!
But they had been very clever, & not too greedy; & I had not found out.
Ever since I moved they must have been busy burrowing all the way to my
Cliff, boring, banging & blasting (as quietly as they could). At last they
had reached my new cellars, & the sight of the Hornby things was too
much for them & they took all they could. I daresay they were also still
angry with the P.B. Also they thought we couldn't get at them. But
I sent my patent green luminous smoke down the tunnel & P.B. blew &
blew it with our enormous kitchen bellows. They simply shrieked &
rushed out the other (cave) end. But there were Red Gnomes there. I had
specially sent for them — a few of the real old families are still in Norway.
They captured hundreds of goblins, & chased many more out into the
snow (which they hate). We made them show us where they had hidden
things, or bring them all back again & by Monday we had got practically
everything back. The Gnomes are still dealing with the goblins, & promise
there won't be one left by New Year — but I am not so sure: they will crop
up again in a century or so, I expect.

We have had a rush; but dear old CBC & his sons & the
Gnome-ladies helped, so that we are now very well forward & all packed.
I hope there is not the faintest smell of goblin about any of your things.
They have all been well aired. There are still a few railway things
missing but I hope you will have what you want. I am not able to carry
quite as much toy-cargo as usual this year, as I am taking a good deal of
food and clothes (useful stuff): there are far too many people in your
land, & others, who are hungry & cold this winter. I am glad that with
you the weather is warmish. It's not warm here. We have had
tremendous icy winds & terrific snow-storms & my old house is quite
buried. But I am feeling very well, better than ever, & though
my hand wobbles with a pen, partly because I don't like writing as much
as drawing (which I learned first), I don't think it's so wobbly this
year.

The P.B. got your father's scribble to-day, & was very
puzzled by it. He thought the written side was meant for him. I told
him it looked like old lecture-notes, & he laughed. He says he thinks
Oxford is quite a mad place if people lecture such stuff; but I don't
suppose anybody listens to it. The other side pleased him better.
He said: "At any rate those boys' father tried to draw bears — though they
aren't good. Of course it is all nonsense, but I will answer it".

So he made up an alphabet from the marks in the caves. He says
it is much nicer than the ordinary letters, or than Runes, or Polar letters,
and suits his paw better. He writes them with the tail of his pen-holder!
He has sent a short letter to you in this alphabet —— to wish you a

P.T.O.

91

at home. Goblins anyway dislike green, so I found them useful.

You see, when I rescued Polar Bear, we hadn't finished the adventures. At the beginning of last week we went into the cellars to get up the stuff for England. I said to Polar Bear, "Somebody has been disarranging things here!"

"Paksu and Valkotukka, I expect," he said. But it wasn't. Next day things were much worse, especially among the railway things, lots of which seemed to be missing. I ought to have guessed, and Polar Bear anyway, ought to have mentioned his guess to me.

Last Saturday we went down and found nearly everything had disappeared out of the main cellar! Imagine my state of mind! Nothing hardly to send to anybody, and too little time to get or make enough new stuff.

North Polar Bear said, "I smell goblin strong." Of course, it was obvious: – they love mechanical toys (though they quickly smash them, and want more and more and more); and practically all the Hornby things had gone! Eventually we found a large hole (but not big enough for us), leading to a tunnel, behind some packing-cases in the West Cellar.

As you will expect we rushed off to find Cave Bear, and we went back to the caves. We soon understood the queer noises. It was plain the goblins long ago had burrowed a tunnel from the caves to my old home (which was not so far from the end of their hills), and had stolen a good many things.

We found some things more than a hundred years old, even a few parcels still addressed to your great-grand-people! But they had been very clever, and not too greedy, and I had not found out.

Ever since I moved they must have been busy burrowing all the way to my Cliff, boring, banging and blasting (as quietly as they could). At last they had reached my new cellars, and the sight of the Hornby things was too much for them: they took all they could.

I daresay they were also still angry with the Polar Bear. Also they thought we couldn't get at them. But I sent my patent green luminous smoke down the tunnel, and Polar Bear blew and blew it with our enormous kitchen bellows. They simply shrieked and rushed out the other (cave) end.

But there were Red Gnomes there. I had specially sent for them – a few of the real old families are still in Norway. They captured hundreds of goblins, and chased many more out into the snow (which they hate). We made them show us where they had hidden things, or bring them all back again, and by Monday we had got practically everything back. The Gnomes are still dealing with the goblins, and promise there won't be one left by New Year – but I am not so sure: they will crop up again in a century or so, I expect.

We have had a rush; but dear old Cave Bear and his sons and the Gnome-ladies helped; so that we are now very well forward and all packed. I hope there is not the faintest smell of goblin about any of your things. They have all been well aired. There are still a few railway things missing, but I hope you will have what you want. I am not able to carry quite as much toy-cargo as usual this year, as I am taking a good deal of food and clothes (useful stuff): there are far too many people in your land, and others, who are hungry and cold this winter.

I am glad that with you the weather is warmish. It is not warm here. We have had tremendous icy winds and terrific snow-storms, and my old house is quite buried. But I am feeling very well, better than ever, and though my hand wobbles with a pen, partly because I don't like writing as much as drawing (which I learned first), I don't think it is so wobbly this year.

The Polar Bear got your father's scribble to-day, and was very puzzled by it. I told him it looked like old lecture-notes, and he laughed. He says he thinks Oxford is quite a mad place if people lecture such stuff: "but I don't suppose anybody listens to it." The drawings pleased him better. He said: "At any rate those boys' father tried to draw bears – though they aren't good. Of course it is all nonsense, but I will answer it."

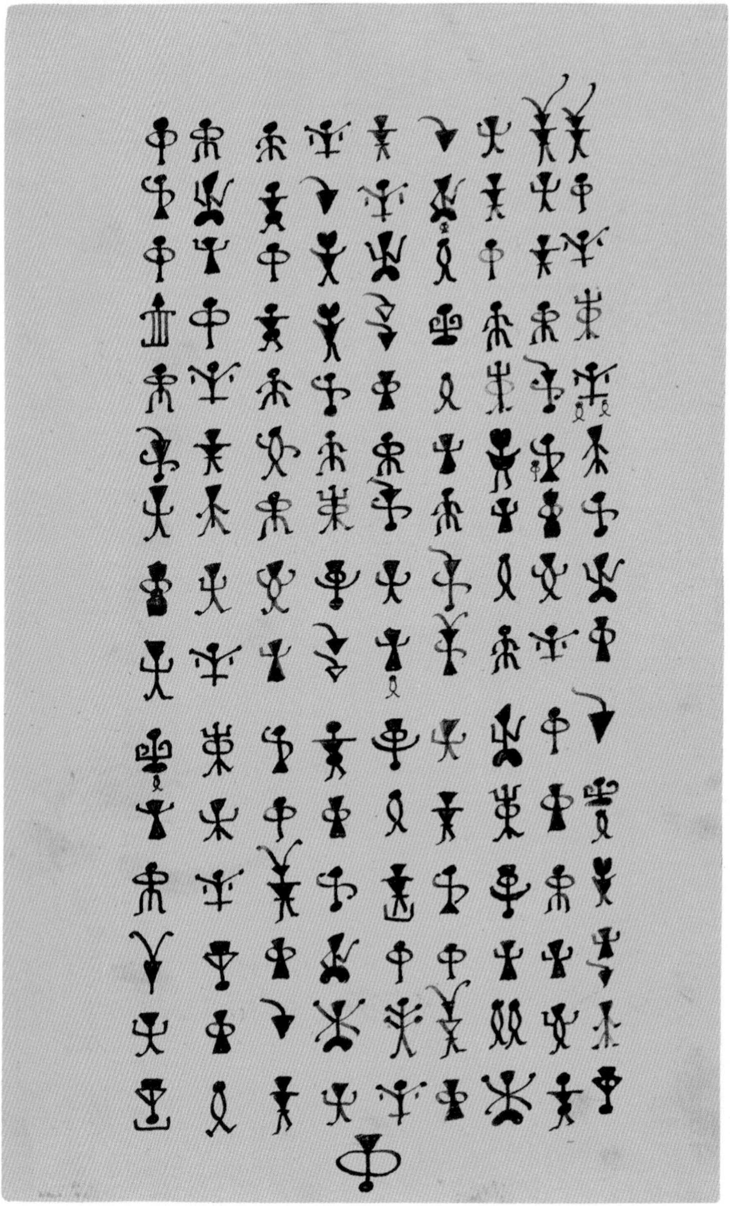

a very Merry Christmas and lots of fun in the New Year and good luck at School. As you are all so clever now (he says) what with Latin & French & Greek you will easily read it and see that P.B. sends much love. *

I am not so sure. But P.B. says that nearly all of it is actually in my letter between the two red stars. (Anyway, I dare say he would send you a copy of his alphabet if you wrote & asked. By the way he writes it in columns from top to bottom not across: don't tell him I gave away his secret).

This is one of my very longest letters. It has been an exciting time. I hope you will like hearing about it. I send you all my love: John, Michael, Christopher, & Priscilla: also Mummy and Daddy and Auntie & all the people in your house. I daresay John will feel he has got to give up stockings now & give way to the many new children that have arrived since he first began to hang his up; but Fr. Th. will not forget him.

Bless you all. Your loving

Nicholas Christmas.

Christmas 1932 *

So he made up an alphabet from the marks in the caves. He says it is much nicer than the ordinary letters, or than Runes, or Polar letters, and suits his paw better. He writes them with the tail of his pen-holder! He has sent a short letter to you in this alphabet – to wish you a very Merry Christmas and lots of fun in the New Year and good luck at School. As you are all so clever now (he says) what with Latin and French and Greek you will easily read it and see that Polar Bear sends much love.

I am not so sure. (Anyway I dare say he would send you a copy of his alphabet if you wrote and asked. By the way he writes it in columns from top to bottom, not across: don't tell him I gave away his secret).

This is one of my very longest letters. It has been an exciting time. I hope you will like hearing about it. I send you all my love: John, Michael, Christopher, and Priscilla: also Mummy and Daddy and Auntie and all the people in your house. I dare say John will feel he has got to give up stockings now and give way to the many new children that have arrived since he first began to hang his up; but Father Christmas will not forget him. Bless you all.

Your loving, Nicholas Christmas.

from
Fr. Xmas

North Pole.
Dec. 2nd. 1933.

Dear People. Very cold here at last. Business has really begun, & we are working hard. I have had a good many letters from you. Thank you. I have made notes of what you want so far but I expect I shall hear more from you yet & I am rather short of messengers — the goblins have — but I haven't time to tell you about our

excitements now. I hope I shall find time to send a letter — later. Give John my love when you see him. I send love to all of you, & a kiss for Priscilla — tell her my beard is quite nice & soft, as I have never shaved. Three weeks to Christmas Eve!

Yrs Father N. Christmas

CHEER VP CHAPS* THE
FUN'S BEGINNING YRS
*also chapter (if that's the feminine) F. B.

1933

Near North Pole
December 2nd 1933

Dear People,

Very cold here at last. Business has really begun, and we are working hard. I have had a good many letters from you. Thank you. I have made notes of what you want so far, but I expect I shall hear more from you yet

By hand.

Mr & Ch. & P. Tolkien
Oxford
England

– I am rather short of messengers – the goblins have—
but I haven't time to tell you about our excitements
now. I hope I shall find time to send a letter later.

Give John my love when you see him. I send love to
all of you, and a kiss for Priscilla – tell her my beard is
quite nice and soft, as I have never shaved.

Three weeks to Christmas Eve!

Yours, Father Nicholas Christmas

**Cheer up, chaps (Also chaplet, if that's the feminine).
The fun's beginning!**

Yours, Polar Bear

Cliff House, near the North Pole
December 21st 1933

My dears

Another Christmas! and I almost thought at one time
(in November) that there would not be one this year.
There would be the 25th of December, of course, but
nothing from your old great-great-etc. grandfather at
the North Pole.

Goblins. The worst attack we have had for centuries.
They have been fearfully wild and angry ever since we
took all their stolen toys off them last year and dosed
them with green smoke. You remember the Red
Gnomes promised to clear all of them out. There was
not one to be found in any hole or cave by New Year's
day. But I said they would crop up again – in a century
or so.

They have not waited so long! They must have
gathered their nasty friends from mountains all over
the world, and been busy all the summer while we
were at our sleepiest. This time we had very little
warning.

Soon after All Saints' Day, Polar Bear got very restless. He now says he smelt nasty smells – but as usual he did not say anything: he says he did not want to trouble me. He really is a nice old thing, and this time he absolutely saved Christmas. He took to sleeping in the kitchen with his nose towards the cellar-door, opening on the main-stairway down into my big stores.

One night, just about Christopher's birthday, I woke up suddenly. There was squeaking and spluttering in the room and a nasty smell – in my own best

Cliff House
near the North Pole.
✳ December 21st ✳
1933

My dears

Another Christmas! and I almost thought at one time (in November) that there would not be one this year. There would be the 25th of Dec. of course, but nothing from your old great-great-great-etc. grandfather at the North Pole. My pictures tell you part of the story. **Goblins** The worst attack we have had for centuries. They have been fearfully wild and angry ever since we took all their stolen toys off them last year & dosed them with green smoke. You remember the Red Gnomes promised to clear all of them out. There was not one to be found in any hole or cave by New Year's day. But I said they would crop up again —in'a century or so. They have not waited so long! They must have gathered their nasty friends from mountains all over the world & been busy all the summer while we were at our sleepiest. This time we had very little warning. Soon after All Saints' Day PB got very restless. He now says he smelt nasty smells — but as usual he did not say anything: he says he did not want to trouble me. He really is a nice old thing, & this time he absolutely saved Christmas. He took to sleeping in the kitchen with his nose towards the cellar-door, opening on the main-stairway down into my big stores.

One night just about Christopher's birthday, I woke up suddenly. There was squeaking and splittering in the room & a nasty smell — in my own best green & purple room that I had

green and purple room that I had just had done up most beautifully. I caught sight of a wicked little face at the window. Then I really was upset, for my window is high up above the cliff, and that meant there were bat-riding goblins about – which we haven't seen since the goblin-war in 1453, that I told you about.

I was only just quite awake, when a terrific din began far downstairs – in the store-cellars. It would take too long to describe, so I have tried to draw a picture of what I saw when I got down – after treading on a goblin on the mat.

Only ther was more like 1000 goblins than 15.

(But you could hardly expect me to draw 1000). Polar Bear was squeezing, squashing, trampling, boxing and kicking goblins skyhigh, and roaring like a zoo, and the goblins were yelling like engine whistles. He was splendid.

Say no more – I enjoyed it immensely!

Well, it is a long story. The trouble lasted for over a fortnight, and it began to look as if I should never be able to get my sleigh out this year. The goblins had set part of the stores on fire and captured several gnomes, who sleep down there on guard, before Polar Bear and some more gnomes came in – and killed 100 before I arrived.

just had done up most beautifully. I caught sight of a wicked little face at the window. Then I really *was* upset, for my window is high up above the cliff, & that meant there bat-riding goblins about — which we haven't seen since the goblin-war in 1453, that I told you about. I was only just quite awake, when a terrific din began far down the stairs —in the store-cellars. It would take too long to describe, so I have tried to draw a picture of what I saw when I got down — after treading on a goblin on the mat. **ONLY THERE WAS MORE LIKE 1000 GOBLINS THAN 15** F.F. (But you could hardly expect me to draw 1000.) P.B. was squeezing, squashing, trampling, boxing and kicking goblins sky-high & roaring like a zoo & the goblins were yelling like engine whistles. He was splendid. [**SAY NO MORE — I ENJOYED IT IM-MENSELY**] Well it is a long story. The trouble lasted for over a fortnight & it began to look as if I should never be able to get my sleigh out this year. The goblins had set part of the stores on fire and captured several gnomes who sleep down there on guard before (& some more gnomes came in — and killed 100 before I arrived. So when we had put the fire out — and cleared the cellars and house (I can't think what they were doing in my room, unless they were trying to set fire to my bed) the trouble went on. The ground was black with goblins under the moon when we looked out, and they had broken up my stables and gone off with the reindeer. I had to blow my golden trumpet (which I have not done for many years) to summon all my friends. There were several battles — every night they used to attack and set fire in the stores — before we got the upper hand & I am afraid quite a lot of my dear elves got hurt. Fortunately we have not lost much except my best sledge (gold and silver) and packing papers and holly-boxes. I am now rather short of these; and I have been very short of messengers. Lots of my people are still away (I hope they will come back safe) chasing the goblins out of my land, those that are left alive. They have rescued all my reindeer. We are quite happy & settled again now, & I feel much safer. It really will be centuries before we get another goblin-trouble. Thanks to

105

PB, & the gnomes, there can't be very many left at all.
AND FR.C. I WISH I COULD DRAW OR
HAD TIME TO TRY — YOU HAVE NO IDEA
WHAT THE OLD MAN CAN DOO! LITENING
AND FIERWORKS AND THUNDER OF GUNS!

PB certainly has been busy, helping double helps — but he has
mixed up some of the girls things with the boys' in his hurry. We
hope we have got all sorted out — but if you hear of any one getting
a doll when they wanted an engine, you will knowd why.
Actually PB tells me from Survans we did lose a lot of
railway stuff — goblins always go for that — and what we got
back was damaged and will have to be repainted. It
will be a busy summer next year.

Now a merry Christmas to you all once again. I
hope you will all have a very happy time. Us
will find that I have taken notice of your letters, & sent you
what you wanted. I don't think my pictures are very
good this year — though I took quite a time over them
(at least two minutes). PB says "I don't see that a lot of stars
& pictures of goblins in your bed room are so frightfully merry".
Still I hope you won't mind. It is rather good of PB kicking
really. Anyway I send lots of love

Yours ever and annually
Father N. Christmas.

Even when we had put the fire out and cleared the cellars and house (I can't think what they were doing in my room, unless they were trying to set fire to my bed) the trouble went on. The ground was black with goblins under the moon when we looked out, and they had broken up my stables and gone off with the reindeer.

I had to blow my golden trumpet (which I have not done for many years) to summon all my friends. There were several battles – every night they used to attack and set fire in the stores – before we got the upper hand, and I am afraid quite a lot of my dear elves got hurt.

Fortunately we have not lost much except my best string, (gold and silver) and packing papers and holly-boxes. I am very short of these: and I have been very short of messengers. Lots of my people are still away (I hope they will come back safe) chasing the goblins out of my land, those that are left alive.

They have rescued all my reindeer. We are quite happy and settled again now, and feel much safer. It really will be centuries before we get another goblin-trouble. Thanks to Polar Bear and the gnomes, there can't be very many left at all.

And Father Christmas. I wish I could draw or had time to try – you have no idea what the old man can doo! Litening and fierworks and thunder of guns!

Polar Bear certainly has been busy helping, and double help – but he has mixed up some of the girls' things with the boys' in his hurry. We hope we have got all sorted out – but if you hear of anyone getting a doll when they wanted an engine, you will know why. Actually Polar Bear tells me I am wrong – we did lose a lot of railway stuff – goblins always go for that – and what we got back was damaged and will have to be repainted. It will be a busy summer next year.

Now, a merry Christmas to you all once again. I hope you will all have a very happy time; and will find that I have taken notice of your letters and sent you what you wanted. I don't think my pictures are very good this year – though I took quite a time over them (at least two minutes). Polar Bear says, "I don't see that a lot of stars and pictures of goblins in your bedroom are so frightfully merry." Still I hope you won't mind. It is rather good of Polar Bear kicking, really. Anyway I send lots of love.

Yours ever and annually
Father Nicholas Christmas.

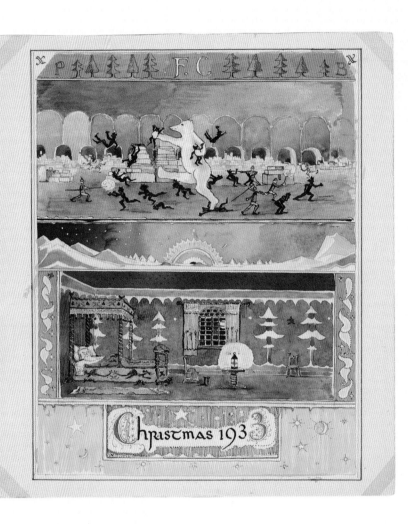

1934

At once   Urgent   Express!

My dear Christopher

Thank you! I am awake – and have been a long while.
But my post office does not really open ever until
Michaelmas. I shall not be sending my messengers out
regularly this year until about October 15th. There is
a good deal to do up here. Your telegram – that is why
I have sent an express reply – and letter and Priscilla's
were found quite by accident: not by a messenger
but by Bellman (I don't know how he got that name
because he never rings any; he is my chimney inspector
and always begins work as soon as the first fires are lit).

Very much love to you and Priscilla. (The Polar Bear,
if you remember him, is still fast asleep, and quite thin
after so much fasting. He will soon cure that. I shall
tickle his ribs and wake him up soon; and then he will
eat several months' breakfast all in one).

More love, your loving Father Christmas

!! To messenger: Deliver at once and don't stop
on the way!!

My dear C.

Thank you! I am awake — & have been a long while. ∴ But my post office does not — really — open ever until Michaelmas. I shall not be sending my messengers out regularly this year until about October 15th. There is a good deal to do up here. Your telegram — that is why I have sent an express reply — & letter of Priscilla's (does she really spell it that way?) were found quite by accident: not by a messenger, but by Bellman (I don't know how he got that name because he never rings any; he is my chimney inspector

& always begins work as soon as the first fires are lit). Very much love to you and P. (The P.B. if you remember him, is still fast asleep & quite thin after so much fasting. He will soon cure that. I shall tickle his ribs & wake him up soon; & then he will eat several months' breakfast — all in one.) More love.

Your loving Fr.

1934

"To messenger: Deliver at once & don't stop on the way!"

Cliff House,
North Pole
Christmas Eve. 1934

My dear Christopher

Thank you very much for your many letters. I have not
had time this year to write you so long a letter as 1932
and 1933, but nothing at all exciting has happened.
I hope I have pleased you with the things I am
bringing and that they are near enough to your lists.

Very little news: after the frightful business of last year there has not been even a smell of goblin for 200 miles round. But, as I said it would, it took us far into the summer to repair all the damage, and we lost a lot of sleep and rest.

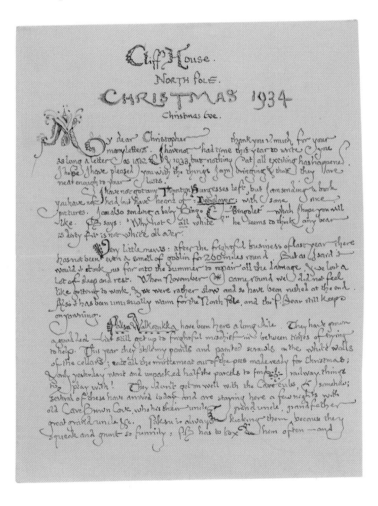

Christmas 1934

114

When November came round we did not feel like getting to work, and we were rather slow and so have been rushed at the end. Also it has been unusually warm for the North Pole, and the Polar Bear still keeps on yawning.

Paksu and Valkotukka have been here a long while. They have grown a good deal – but still get up to frightful mischief in between times of trying to help. This year they stole my paints and painted scrawls on the white walls of the cellars; ate all the mincemeat out of the pies made ready for Christmas; and only yesterday went and unpacked half the parcels to find railway things to play with!

They don't get on well with the Cave cubs, somehow; several of these have arrived today and are staying here a few nights with old Cave Brown Cave, who is their uncle, granduncle, grandfather, great granduncle, etc. Paksu is always kicking them because they squeak and grunt so funnily: Polar Bear has to box him often – and a 'box' from Polar Bear is no joke.

As there are no Goblins about, and as there is no wind, and so far much less snow than usual, we are going to have a great boxing-day party ourselves – out of doors. I shall ask 100 elves and red gnomes, lots of polar cubs, cave-cubs, and snowbabies, and of course, Paksu and Valkotukka, and Polar Bear and Cave Bear and his nephews (etc.) will be there.

a box from F.C. is no joke. As there are no Goblins about, and as there is no wind, & so far much less snow than usual, we are going to have a great boxing-day party ourselves — out of doors. I shall ask 100 elves & red gnomes, lots of polar cubs, cave-cubs and snow-babies & of course P.B. and C.B. and his nephews (eh) will be there.

We have brought a tree all the way from Norway and planted it in a pool of ice. My picture gives you no idea of its size. or of the loveliness of its magic lights of different colours. We tried them yesterday evening to see if they were all right — See picture. If you see a bright glow in the North you will know what it is! The tree-ish things behind are snowplants, and piled masses of snow made into ornamental shapes — they are purple and black because of darkness & shadow. The coloured things in front is a special edging to the ice-pool — and it is made of a real coloured & icing. P.B. are already nibbling at it, though they should not — till the party.

P.B. started to draw this to help me, as I was busy — but he dropped such blots — enormous ones — hold it up to the light and you will see where I had to come to the rescue. P.B. not very good this year. Never mind: perhaps better next year. I hope you will like your presents & be very happy. Your loving

F. Christmas.

P.S. I really can't remember exactly in what year I was born. I doubt if anyone knows. I am always changing my own mind about it. Anyway it was 1934 years ago or jolly nearly that. Bless you!

F.C.

P.B. LOVE
P.B. Give my love to Mick & John.
BISY THANKS

We have brought a tree all the way from Norway and planted it in a pool of ice. My picture gives you no idea of its size, or of the loveliness of its magic lights of different colours. We tried them yesterday evening to see if they were all right. If you see a bright glow in the North you will know what it is!

Behind the tree are snowplants, and piled masses of snow made into ornamental shapes – they are purple and black because of darkness and shadow. There is also a special edging to the ice-pool – and it is made of real coloured icing. Paksu and Valkotukka are already nibbling at it, though they should not – till the party.

Polar Bear started to draw this to help me, as I was busy, but he dropped such blots – enormous ones. I had to come to the rescue. Not very good this year. Never mind: perhaps better next year.

I hope you will like your presents and be very happy.

Your loving
Father Christmas.

PS I really can't remember exactly in what year I was born. I doubt if anyone knows. I am always changing my own mind about it. Anyway it was 1934 years ago or jolly nearly that. Bless you! FC
PPS Give my love to Mick and John.

Polar Bear LOVE BISY THANKS

December 24 1934

Dear Priscilla,

Thank you for nice letters. Lots of love. I hope you will be quite well & enjoy the things I am bringing. Can you read this yourself yet: it is my best writing?

Polar bear sends love. He is glad you have called your bear Bingo: he thinks it is a jolly name, but he thinks bears ought to be white all over. I send a picture with Christopher's letter which is for both of you.

Your loving,
Fr. Christmas

Love
Bisy
Thanks P.B

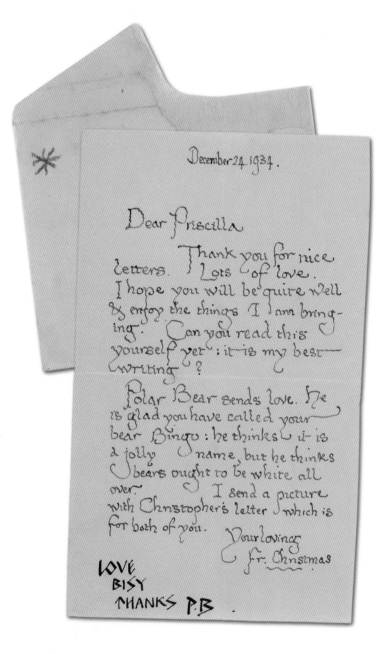

December 24 1934.

Dear Priscilla

Thank you for nice letters. Lots of love. I hope you will be quite well & enjoy the things I am bringing. Can you read this yourself yet: it is my best writing?

Polar Bear sends love. He is glad you have called your bear Bingo: he thinks it is a jolly name, but he thinks bears ought to be white all over. I send a picture with Christopher's letter which is for both of you.

Your loving
Fr. Christmas

LOVE
BISY
THANKS P.B.

119

1935

December 24 1935
North Pole

My dear Children

Here we are again. Christmas seems to come round pretty soon again: always much the same and always different. No ink this year and no water, so no painted pictures; also very cold hands, so very wobbly writing.

Last year it was very warm, but this year it is frightfully cold – snow, snow, snow, and ice. We have been simply buried, messengers have got lost and found themselves in Nova Scotia, if you know where that is, instead of in Scotland; and PB, if you know who that is, could not get home.

This is a picture of my house about a week ago before we got the reindeer sheds dug out. We had to make a tunnel to the front door. There are only three windows upstairs shining through holes – and there is steam where the snow is melting off the dome and roof.

This is a view from my bedroom window. Of course, snow coming down is not blue – but blue is cold: You can understand why your letters were slow in going. I hope I got them all, and anyway that the right things arrive for you.

Poor old PB, if you know who I mean, had to go away soon after the snow began last month. There was some trouble in his family, and Paksu and Valkotukka were ill. He is very good at doctoring anybody but himself.

But it is a dreadfully long way over the ice and snow – to North Greenland I believe. And when he got there he could not get back. So I have been rather held up, especially as the Reindeer stables and the outdoor store sheds are snowed over.

I have had to have a lot of Red Elves to help me. They are very nice and great fun; but although they are very quick they don't get on fast. For they turn everything

December 24 1935

North Pole

My Dear Children:

Here we are again. Christmas seems to come round pretty soon again: always much the same and always different. NO INK this year and no water, so no painted pictures; also very cold hands, so very wobbly writing. Last year it was very warm, but this year it is frightfully cold — snow, snow, snow and ice. We have been simply buried, messengers have got lost and found themselves in Nova Scotia, if you know where that is, instead of in Scotland; and P.B. if you know who that is, could not get home. This is a picture of

SILLY

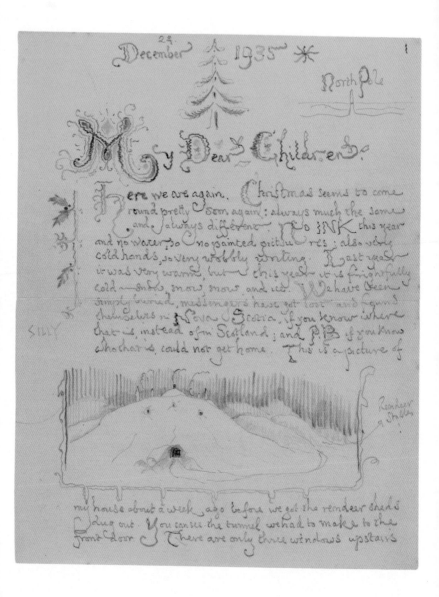

Reindeer Stables

my house about a week ago before we got the reindeer sheds dug out. You can see the tunnel we had to make to the front door. There are only three windows upstairs

122

shining through like — but you can see steam where
the Snow is melting off the dome and roof.
This a view from my bedroom window. Of course snow

coming down is not blue — but blue is cold. You can
understand why your letters were slow in coming

SILLY
AGAIN

though I got them all, and anyway that the right
things arrive for you. Poor old P.B., I you who
I mean, had to go away
soon after the snow began
last month. There was some
trouble in his family, and some
of Valkotukka were ill. He —

very good at doctoring anybody but himself. But it
it's a dreadful long way over the ice and snow
to North Greenland, I believe. And when he got
there he could not get back. So I have been rather
held up, especially as the Reindeer stables and the outdoor
store sheds are snowed over. I have had to have a

lots of Red Elves to help me. They are very nice
& great fun; but although they are very quick they
don't get on fast. For they turn everything into a
game. Even digging snow. And they will play with

into a game. Even digging snow. And they will play with the toys they are supposed to be packing.

PB, if you remember him, did not get back until Friday December 13th – so that proved a lucky day for me after all!

(HEAR HEAR!)

Even he had to wear a sheepskin coat and red gloves for his paws. And he had got a hood on and red gloves. He thinks he looks rather like Rye St Anthony. But of course he does not very much. Anyway he carries things in his hood – he brought home his sponge and soap in it!

He says that we have not seen the last of the goblins – in spite of the battles in 1933. They won't dare to come into my land yet; but for some reason they are breeding again and multiplying all over the world. Quite a nasty outbreak. But there are not so many in England, he says. I expect I shall have trouble with them soon.

I have given my elves some new magic sparkler spears that will scare them out of their wits. It is now December 24th and they have not appeared this year – and practically everything is packed up and ready. I shall be starting soon

I send you all – John and Michael and Christopher and Priscilla – my love and good wishes this Christmas:

the toys they are supposed to be packing.

P.B., if you remember him, did not get back until Sunday December the 13th — so that proved a lucky day for me (HEAR HEAR!) after all. Even he had to wear a sheepskin coat & red gloves for his paws, and he had on red a hood on and red gloves. He thinks he looks rather like but of course Rye St Anthony he does not very

much. Anyway he carries things in his hood — he brought Shomé his sponge and soap in it!

He says that we have not seen the last of the goblins — nor of the battles in 1933. They won't dare to come into my land yet; but for some reason they are breeding again and multiplying all over the world. Quite a nasty outbreak! But there are not so many in England, he says. I expect I shall have trouble with them soon. I have given my elves

Some new magic sparkler spears that will scare them out of their wits. It is now December 24 and they have not appeared this year — and practically everything is packed up and ready. I shall be starting soon

1935

I send you all — John & Michael & 'topher & Priscilla — my love and good wishes this Xmas: tons of good wishes. Pass on a few if you don't want them all!

Polar Bear (in case you don't know what P.B is) sends love to you — and to the Bingos and to Orange Teddy and 16 Jubilee (O yes I learn lots of news even in Snowy weather)

My messengers will be about until the New Year if you want to write and tell me everything was all right. I hope you enjoy the

PANTOMIME

Your loving

Father Christmas

P.S P & I are well again. Only Bumps. They will beat my big party on St Stephens Day with other polar cubs, cave cubs, snowbabies, elves, and all the rest.

STUPID JOKE

✳
PB

tons of good wishes. Pass on a few if you don't want them all! Polar Bear (in case you don't know what PB is) sends love to you – and to the Bingos and to Orange Teddy and to Jubilee. (O yes I learn lots of news even in Snowy weather). My messengers will be about until the New Year if you want to write and tell me everything was all right.

I hope you enjoy the pantomime

Your loving
Father Christmas

PS Paksu and Valkotukka are well again. Only mumps. They will be at my big party on St Stephen's Day with other polar cubs, cave cubs, snowbabies, elves, and all the rest.

Cliff House.
North Pole
Wednesday Dec 23rd
1936

My dear Children

I am sorry I cannot send you a
long letter to thank you for yours, but
I am sending you a picture which will explain
a good deal. It is a good thing your
changed lists arrived before these dateful
events, or I could not have done anything
about it. I do hope you will like what I am
bringing and will forgive any mistakes, & I
hope nothing will still be wet! I am
still so shaky and upset. I am getting one of
my elves to write a bit more about things.
I send very much love to you all.

Father C. says you will want to hear some news. PB has been quite
good — or had been — though he has been rather tired. So has F.C. I think
the Christmas business is getting rather too much for them. So a lot of us,
red and green elves, have gone to live permanently at Cliff House, and be
trained in the packing business. It was PB's idea. He also invented the
number system, so that every child that F.C. deals with has a number
and we elves learn them all by heart, and all the addresses. That saves

1936

Cliff House
North Pole
Wednesday Dec. 23rd 1936

My dear Children

I am sorry I cannot send you a long letter to thank you for yours, but I am sending you a picture which will explain a good deal. It is a good thing your changed lists arrived before these awful events, or I could not have done anything about it. I do hope you will like what I am bringing and will forgive any mistakes, and I hope nothing will still be wet! I am still so shaky and upset, I am getting one of my elves to write a bit more about things.

I send very much love to you all.

Father Christmas says you will want to hear some news. Polar Bear has been quite good – or had been – though he has been rather tired. So has Father Christmas; I think the Christmas business is getting rather too much for them.

So a lot of us, red and green elves, have gone to live permanently at Cliff House, and be trained in the packing business. It was Polar Bear's idea. He

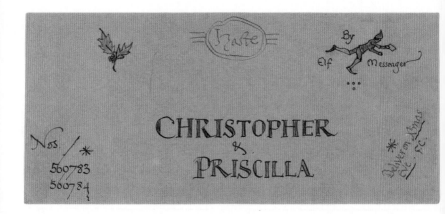

CHRISTOPHER
&
PRISCILLA

also invented the number system, so that every child that Father Christmas deals with has a number and we elves learn them all by heart, and all the addresses. That saves a lot of writing.

So many children have the same name that every packet used to have the address as well. Polar Bear said: "I am going to have a record year and help Father Christmas to get so forward we can have some fun ourselves on Christmas day."

We all worked hard, and you will be surprised to hear that every single parcel was packed and numbered by Saturday (December 19th). Then Polar Bear said "I am tired out: I am going to have a hot bath, and go to bed early!"

Well you can guess what happened. Father Christmas was taking a last look round in the English Delivery Room about 10 o'clock when water poured through the ceiling and swamped everything: it was soon 6 inches deep on the floor. Polar Bear had simply got into the bath with both taps running and gone fast asleep with one hind paw on the overflow. He had been asleep two hours when we woke him.

a lot of writing. So many children have the same name that every packet used to have the address as well. P.B. said: I am going to have a record year and help F.C. to get so forward we can have some fun ourselves on Xmas day. We all worked hard, and you will be surprised to hear that every single parcel was packed and numbered by Saturday last (Dec 19). Then P.B. said 'I am tired out: I am going to have a hot bath and go to bed early.' Well you can see what happened. F.C. was taking a last look round in the English Delivery Room about 10 o'clock when water poured through the ceiling and swamped everything: it was soon 6 ins. deep on the floor. P.B. had simply got into the bath with both taps running and gone fast asleep with one hind paw on the overflow. He had been asleep two hours when we woke him. F.C. was really angry. But P.B. only said: 'I did have a jolly dream. I dreamt I was diving off a melting iceberg and chasing seals." He said later when he saw the damage: "Well there are some things: those children at Northpole Road (he always says that) Oxford may lose some of their presents, but they will have a letter worth having this year. They can see a joke, even if none of you can!" That made F.C. angrier, and P.B. said: "Well, draw a picture of it, and ask them if it is funny or not." So F.C. has. But he has begun to think it funny (although very annoying) himself, now we have cleared up the mess, & got the English presents repacked again. Just in time. We are all rather tired, so please excuse scrawly writing—

Yrs. Ilbereth, Secretary to F.t Christmas

VERY SORRY. BEEN BIZY. CAN'T FIND THAT
ALPHABET. WILL I LOOK AFTER CHRISTMAS
AND POST IT   YRS. P.B.

You will find two snapshots in this letter. Give them back to your Mother. I hoped she has not missed them. One of my selves borrowed them. You will find out what for

Yrs F.C.

Father Christmas was really angry. But Polar Bear only said: "I did have a jolly dream. I dreamt I was diving off a melting iceberg and chasing seals."

He said later when he saw the damage: "Well there is one thing: those children at Northpole Road, Oxford (he always says that) may lose some of their presents, but they will have a letter worth hearing this year. They can see a joke, even if none of you can!"

That made Father Christmas angrier, and Polar Bear said: "Well, draw a picture of it and ask them if it is funny or not." So Father Christmas has. But he has begun to think it funny (although very annoying) himself, now we have cleared up the mess, and got the English presents repacked again. Just in time. We are all rather tired, so please excuse scrawly writing.

Yours, Ilbereth, Secretary to Father Christmas

Very sorry. Been bizy. Can't find that alphabet. Will look after Christmas and post it. Yours, Polar Bear.

I have found it. I send you a copy. You needn't fill in black parts if you don't want to. It takes rather long to rite but I think it is rather clever.

Still bizy. Father Christmas sez I can't have a bath till next year.

Love tou yo both bicause you see jokes

Polar Bear

I got into hot water didn't I? Ha! Ha!

I HAVE FOUND IT. I SEND YOU
A COPY. YOU NEEDNT. FILL IN
BLACK PARTS IF YOU DONT
WANT TO. IT TAKES RATHER
LONG TO RITE BUT I THINK
IT IS RATHER CLEVER.

STILL BIZY. F.C. SEZ I CANT
HAVE A BATH TILL NEXT YEAR.
LOVE TOU YO BOTH BICAUSE
YOU SEE JOKES

B.B.

I GOT INTO HOT WATER
DIDNT I? HA! HA! P.B.

134

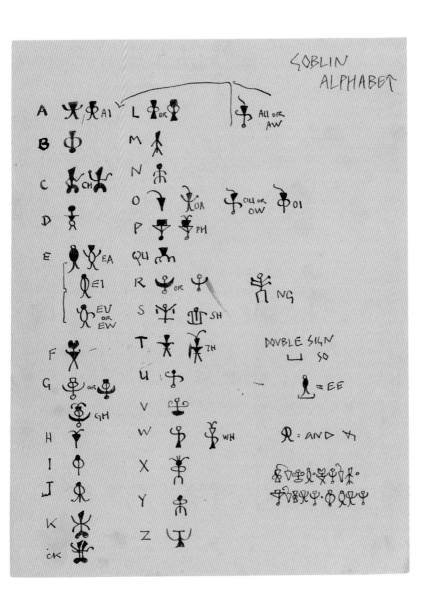

GOBLIN ALPHABET

135

1937

Cliff House,
North Pole
Christmas 1937

My dear Christopher and Priscilla, and other old
friends in Oxford: here we are again!

Of course I am always here (when not travelling), but
you know what I mean. Christmas again. I believe it is
17 years since I started to write to you. I wonder if you

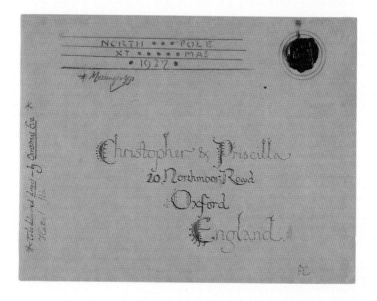

Cliff House
North Pole
∘ Christmas 1937 ∘

My dear Christopher and
Priscilla, and other old friends
at 20 Northmoor Road, Oxford: here we are again!
Of course I am always here (when not travelling) but you know what I mean.
Christmas again. I believe it is 17 years since I started to write to you. I wonder
if you have still got all my letters? I have not been able to keep quite all yours, but
I have got some from every year. We had quite a fright this year: no letters came from
you. Then one day early in December I sent a messenger who used to go to Oxford a lot.
But had not been there for a long while, and he said: 'Their house is
empty and everything is sold.' I was afraid something had happened, or that you had
all gone to school in some other town, and your Father and mother had
moved. Of course, I know now: the messenger had been to your old house next
door! He complained that all the windows were shut and the chimneys all
blocked up. I was very glad indeed to get Priscilla's first letter, and your
two nice letters, and useful lists and hints, since Christopher came back.
I quite understand that School makes it difficult for you to write like you
used. And of course I have new children coming on my lists each year
so that I don't get less busy.

Tell your Father I am sorry about his eyes and throat: I once had my eyes
very bad from Snow-blindness, which comes from looking at sunlit snow. But
I got better. I hope Priscilla and your Mother and everyone else will be well on
Dec. 25. I am afraid I have not had any time to draw you a picture this year.
You see I strained my hand moving heavy boxes in the 'cellars'. Ha ha
(this: you see) have read your letter in November, and could not start

my letters until later than usual, and my hand still gets tired quickly. But Ilbereth — one of the cleverest Elves (who I took on as a see Intromnot Long ago — is becoming very good. He can write several alphabets now Arctic, Latin (that is Ordinary European like yours), Greek, Russian, Runes, and of course Elvish. His writing is a bit thin and slanting — he has a very slender hand — and his drawing a bit scratchy, I think. He has done you what he calls a picture diary. I hope it will do. He won't use paints he says he's a secretary and so only uses ink (and pencil). He is going to finish this letter for me as I have to do some others. So I will now send you lots of love, & I do hope that I have chosen the best things out of your suggestion lists. I was going to send Hobbits — I am sending away loads (mostly second editions) which I sent for only a few days ago — but I thought you would have lots, so I am sending another Oxford fairy-story. Lots and Lots of Love. Father Christmas

· 1937 ·

Dear Children: I am Ilbereth. I have written to you before. I am finishing for Father Christmas. Shall I tell you about my pictures? Polar Bear and Valkotukka and Paksu are always lazy after Christmas or rather after the St Stephens Day party. F.C. is ringing for breakfast in vain. Another day when P.B. as usual, was late Paksu threw a bath-sponge full of icy water on his face. P.B. chased him all round the house and round the garden and then forgave him, because he had not caught Paksu, but had found a huge appetite. We had terrible weather at the end of winter and actually had rain. We could not go out for days. I have drawn P.B. and his nephews when they did venture out. Paksu and V. have never gone away. They like it so much that they have begged to stay. It was much too warm at the North Pole this year. A large lake formed at the bottom of the Cliff, and left the N. Pole standing on an island. I have drawn a view looking South, so the Cliffs on the other side. It was about mid summer. The N.P.B his nephews and lots of Polar cubs used to come and bathe. Also seals. N.P.B took to trying to paddle a boat or canoe, but he fell in so often that the seals thought he liked it, and used to get under the boat and tip it up. That made him annoyed. The sport did not last long as the water froze again early in August. Then we began to begin to think of this Christmas. In my picture F.Christmas is dividing up the lists and giving me my special lot — you are in it, that is why your numbers are on the board. N.P.B of course always pretends to be managing everything: that's why he is pointing, but I am really listening to F.C. and I am saluting him not N.P.B.

NOT TRUE

RUDE LIANNE ERRAND BOY

have still got all my letters? I have not been able to keep quite all yours, but I have got some from every year.

We had quite a fright this year. No letters came from you. Then one day early in December I sent a messenger who used to go to Oxford a lot but had not been there for a long while, and he said: "Their house is empty and everything is sold." I was afraid something had happened, or that you had all gone to school in some other town, and your father and mother had moved. Of course, I know now; the messenger had been to your old house next door! He complained that all the windows were shut and the chimneys all blocked up.

I was very glad indeed to get Priscilla's first letter, and your two nice letters, and useful lists and hints, since Christopher came back. I quite understand that School makes it difficult for you to write like you used. And of course I have new children coming on my lists each year so that I don't get less busy.

Tell your father I am sorry about his eyes and throat: I once had my eyes very bad from snow-blindness, which comes from looking at sunlit snow. But it got better. I hope Priscilla and your Mother and everyone else will be well on Dec. 25. I am afraid I have not had any time to draw you a picture this year. You see I strained my hand moving heavy boxes in the cellars in November, and could not start my letters until later than usual, and my hand still gets tired quickly. But

Ilbereth – one of the cleverest Elves who I took on as a secretary not long ago – is becoming very good.

He can write several alphabets now – Arctic, Latin (that is ordinary European like you use), Greek, Russian, Runes, and of course Elvish. His writing is a bit thin and slanting – he has a very slender hand – and his drawing is a bit scratchy, I think. He won't use paints – he says he is a secretary and so only uses ink (and pencil). He is going to finish this letter for me, as I have to do some others.

So I will now send you lots of love, and I do hope that I have chosen the best things out of your suggestion lists. I was going to send 'Hobbits' – I am sending away loads (mostly second editions) which I sent for only a few days ago) – but I thought you would have lots, so I am sending another Oxford Fairy Story.

Lots and Lots of Love, Father Christmas

Dear Children:

I am Ilbereth. I have written to you before. I am finishing for Father Christmas. Shall I tell you about my pictures? Polar Bear and Valkotukka and Paksu are always lazy after Christmas, or rather after the St Stephen's Day party. Father Christmas is ringing for breakfast in vain. Another day when Polar Bear, as usual, was late

not true!

A diary of 1936 to 1937 by Ilbereth.

Nobody wants breakfast after Christmas. N.P.B., P. and V. are tired 1936. (and full).

A sponge is useful for waking up N.P.B. but makes him angry.

Late Spring 1937. Thaw and rain. Going for a nice walk to find a lost sprite.

560723
560784

Midsummer. Great hole appears in ice. Seals come out. N.P.B. takes to boating.

Beginning to think of next Christmas. Ilbereth getting orders from F.C.

Celebrating the Coming of Winter. Bonfire party and Fireworks.

Tobogganing down from Cliff House. Snowboys have a good time.

Today. Dec. 23rd. N.P.B. busy with the tree — before the disaster.

Tomorrow. Starting with the first load.

A Merry Christmas 1937   F.C.

141

Paksu threw a bath-sponge full of icy water on his face. Polar Bear chased him all round the house and round the garden and then forgave him, because he had not caught Paksu, but had found a huge appetite.

We had terrible weather at the end of winter and actually had rain. We could not go out for days. I have drawn Polar Bear and his nephews when they did venture out. Paksu and Valkotukka have never gone away. They like it so much that they have begged to stay.

It was much too warm at the North Pole this year. A large lake formed at the bottom of the Cliff, and left the North Pole standing on an island. I have drawn a view looking South, so the Cliff is on the other side. It was about mid-summer. The North Polar Bear, his nephews and lots of polar cubs used to come and bathe. Also seals. North Polar Bear took to trying to paddle a boat or canoe, but he fell in so often that the seals thought he liked it, and used to get under the boat and tip it up. That made him annoyed.

The sport did not last long as the water froze again early in August. Then we began to begin to think of this Christmas. In my picture Father Christmas is dividing up the lists and giving me my special lot – you are in it.

North Polar Bear of course always pretends to be managing everything: that's why he is pointing, but I am really listening to Father Christmas and I am saluting him not North Polar Bear.

Rude little errand boy.

We had a glorious bonfire and fireworks to celebrate the Coming of Winter and the beginning of real 'Preparations'. The Snow came down very thick in November and the elves and snowboys had several

We had a glorious bonfire and fireworks to celebrate the 'Coming of Winter' and the beginning of real 'Preparations'. The snow came down very thick in November and the elves and snowboys had several tobogganing half-holidays. The polar cubs were not good at it. They fell off, and most of them took to rolling or sliding down just on themselves. Today _____ but this is the best bit. I had just finished my pictures, or I might have drawn it differently. P.B. was being allowed to decorate a big tree in the garden, all by himself and a ladder. Suddenly we heard terrible growly squealy noises. We rushed out to find PB hanging on the tree himself! "You are not a decoration" said F.C.

NEITHER

Anyway I am alright "he shouted. He was. We threw a bucket of water over him which spoilt a lot of the decorations, but saved his fur. The silly old thing had rested the ladder against a branch (instead of the trunk of the tree). Then he thought, "I will just light the candles to see if they are working" although he was told not to. So he climbed to the top of the ladder with a taper. Just then the branch cracked, the ladder slipped on the snow, and PB fell into the tree and caught on some wire;

POOR JOKE

and his fur got caught on fire. Luckily he was rather damp or he might have fizzled. I wonder if roast Polar is good to eat? The last picture is imaginary and not very good. But I hope it will come true. Well if P.B. behaves. I hope you can read my writing. I try to write like dear old F.C. (without the trembles), but I cannot do so well. Ilbereth writes much better. [———] thats some — but F.C. says I write even that too spidery and you would never read it : it is any **A very** merry Christmas to you all. Love Ilbereth.

← NOT AS GOOD AS WELL SPANKED AND FRIED ELF

ᛗᚪ·ᛗᚪᚱᛏ That is Runick. NPB A big hug and lots of love. Enormous thanks for letters. I don't get many, though I work so harrd. I am practising new writing with lovely thick pen. Quicker than Arctic. I invented it. ILBERETH IS CHEKY. HOW ARE THE BINGOS? A MERRY CHRISTMAS NcPoB

Vaksu's nose → mark TB

tobogganing half-holidays. The polar cubs were not good at it. They fell off, and most of them took to rolling or sliding down just on themselves. Today — but this is the best bit, I had just finished my picture, or I might have drawn it differently.

And better!

Polar Bear was being allowed to decorate a big tree in the garden, all by himself and a ladder. Suddenly are heard terrible growly squealy noises. We rushed out to find Polar Bear hanging on the tree himself!

"You are not a decoration," said Father Christmas.
"Anyway, I am alight," he shouted.

He was. We threw a bucket of water over him. Which spoilt a lot of the decorations, but saved his fur. The silly old thing had rested the ladder against a branch (instead of the trunk of the tree). Then he thought, "I will just light the candles to see if they are working," although he was told not to. So he climbed to the tip of the ladder with a taper. Just then the branch cracked, the ladder slipped on the snow, and Polar Bear fell into the tree and caught on some wire; and his fur got caught on fire.

Poor joke.

Luckily he was rather damp or he might have fizzled. I wonder if roast Polar is good to eat?

Not as good as well spanked and fried elf.

The last picture is imaginary and not very good. But I hope it will come true. It will if Polar Bear behaves. I hope you can read my writing. I try to write like dear old Father Christmas (without the trembles), but I cannot do so well. I can write Elvish better:

That is some – but Father Christmas says I write even that too spidery and you would never read it.

Love Ilbereth.

A big hug and lots of love. Enormous thanks for letters. I don't get many, though I work so harrd. I am practising new writing with lovely thick pen. Quicker than Arctick. I invented it.

Ilbereth is cheky. How are the Bingos? A merry Christmas. North Polar Bear

1938

Cliff House,
North Pole
Christmas 1938

My dear Priscilla and all others at your house

Here we are again! Bless me, I believe I said that
before – but after all you don't want Christmas to be
different each year, do you?

I am frightfully sorry that I haven't had the time
to draw any big picture this year, and Ilbereth (my
secretary) has not done one either; but we are all
sending you some rhymes instead. Some of my other
children seem to like rhymes, so perhaps you will.

We have all been very sorry to hear about Christopher.
I hope he is better and will have a jolly Christmas.
I only heard lately when my messengers and letter
collectors came back from Oxford. Tell him to cheer
up – and although he is now growing up and leaving
stockings behind, I shall bring a few things along this
year. Among them is a small astronomy book which
gives a few hints on the use of telescopes – thank you
for telling me he had got one. Dear me! My hand is
shaky – I hope you can read some of this?

Cliff House
— North Pole —
Christmas 1938

My dear Priscilla and all others at your
house. Here we are again! Bless me, I believe
I said that before ——— That after all you don't want
Christmas to be different each year, do you?
I am frightfully sorry that I haven't had the time to draw
any big picture this year, and Ilbereth my secretary has not done
one either; but we are all sending you some rhymes instead.
Some of my other children seem to like rhymes, so perhaps you
will.

We have all been very sorry to hear about Christopher. I hope
he is better, & will have a jolly Christmas. I only heard lately
when my messengers & letter-collectors came back from Oxford.
Tell him to cheer up —— and although he is now growing up & leaving
stockings behind, I shall bring a few things along this year.
Among them is a small astronomy book which gives a few
hints on the use of telescopes —— thank you for telling me he had got
one. Dear me! my hand is shaky - I hope you can read some
of this?

I loved your long letter, with all the amusing pictures.
Give my love to your Bingos and all the other sixty (or more!),
especially Raggles and Fredles and Tinker and Tailor and Jubilee
and Snowball. I hope you will go on writing to me for a long while yet.
Very much love to you —— and lots for Chris —— from

Father Christmas

PTO

147

I loved your long letter, with all the amusing pictures. Give my love to your Bingos and all the other sixty (or more!), especially Raggles and Preddley and Tinker and Tailor and Jubilee and Snowball. I hope you will go on writing to me for a long while yet.

Very much love to you – and lots for Chris – from

Father Christmas

Again this year, my dear Priscilla,
when you're asleep upon your pillow;

Bad rhyme!
That's beaten you!

beside your bed old Father Christmas

[The English language has no rhyme
to Father Christmas: that's why I'm
not very good at making verses.
But what I find a good deal worse is
that girls' and boys' names won't rhyme either
(and bother! either won't rhyme neither).
So please forgive me, dear Priscilla,
if I pretend you rhyme with pillow!]

She won't.

As I was saying –

beside your bed old Father Christmas
(afraid that any creak or hiss must

How's that?

Out!

wake you up) will in a twinkling
fill up your stocking, (I've an inkling
that it belongs, in fact, to pater =
but never mind!) At twelve, or later,
he will arrive – and hopes once more
that he has chosen from his store

I did it.

149

the things you want. You're half past nine;

She is not a clock!

but still I hope you'll drop a line
for some years yet, and won't forget
old Father Christmas and his Pet,
the North Polar Bear (and Polar Cubs
as fat as little butter-tubs),
and snowboys and Elves – in fact the whole
of my household up near the Pole.

Upon my list, made in December,
your number is, if you remember,
fifty six thousand, seven hundred,
and eighty five. It can't be wondered

Weak!

at that I am so busy, when
you think that you are nearly ten,
and in that time my list has grown
by quite ten thousand girls alone,
even when I've subtracted all
the houses where I no longer call!

You all will wonder what's the news;
if all has gone well, and if not who's
to blame; and whether Polar Bear
has earned a mark good, bad, or fair,
for his behaviour since last winter.
Well – first he trod upon a splinter,

150

Rhyme.

Again this year, my dear Priscilla,
when you're asleep upon your pillow;
beside your bed old Father Christmas

BAD rhyme!
that's beaten you!

The English language has no rhyme
to Father Christmas: that's why I'm
not very good at making verses.
But what I find a good deal worse is
that girls' and boys' names won't rhyme either
(and bother! either won't rhyme neither).
So please forgive me, dear Priscilla,
if I pretend you rhyme with pillow!

she won't

As I was saying — beside your bed old Father Christmas
(afraid that any creak or hiss must
wake you up) will in a twinkling
fill up your stocking. I've an inkling

How's that? S.C.
OUT! P.F.

Had to help Fr. C.
here. P.borvill.

that it belongs, in fact, to pater —
but never mind! At twelve, or later,
he will arrive — and hopes once more
that he has chosen from his store
the things you want. You're half past nine;

I did it
she is not a clock!

but still I hope you'll drop a line
for some years yet. I won't forget
old Father Christmas and his Pet,
the N.P.B (and Polar Cubs
as fat as little butter tubs),

blots by P.B.V.

and snowboys and Elves — in fact the whole
of my household up near the Pole.
Upon my list, made in December,
your number is, if you remember,
fifty six thousand, seven hundred,
and eighty five. It can't be wondered

wrak!

at that I am so busy when
you think that you are nearly ten,

151

and in that time my list has grown
by quite ten thousand girls alone,
even when I've subtracted all
the houses where I no longer call!

You all will wonder what's the news,
if all has gone well, and if not who's
to blame; and whether Polar Bear
has earned a mark good, bad, or fair
for his behaviour since last winter.
Well — first he trod upon a splinter,
and went on crutches in November;
and then one cold day in December
he burnt his nose & singed his paws
upon the kitchen grate, because
without the help of tongs he tried
to roast hot chestnuts. 'Wow!' he cried,
and used a pound of butter (best)
to cure the burns. He would not rest,
but on the twenty-third he went
and climbed up on the roof. He meant
to clear the snow away that choked
his chimney up — of course he poked
his legs right through the tiles, & snow
in tons fell on his bed below.
He has broken saucers, cups, and glasses;
and eaten lots of chocolates;
he's dropped large boxes on my toes,
and trodden tin-soldiers flat in rows;
he's over-wound engines and broken springs,
& mixed up different children's things;
he's thumbed new books and burst balloons
& scribbled lots of smudgy Runes
on my best paper, and wiped his feet
on scarves and hankies folded neat ——
And yet he has been, on the whole,
a very kind and willing soul.
He's fetched and carried, counted, packed,
and for a week has never slacked:
he's climbed the cellar-stairs at least
five thousand times — the Dear Old Beast!

[margin notes, in a different hand:]

just rhiming
nonsens :it was
a nail — nasty too

I never did!

I was not given a
chance

you need not
believe all this!

hear! hear!

and went on crutches in November;
and then one cold day in December
he burnt his nose and singed his paws
upon the Kitchen grate, because
without the help of tongs he tried
to roast hot chestnuts. "Wow!" he cried,

I never did!

and used a pound of butter (best)
to cure the burns. He would not rest,

I was not given a chance.

but on the twenty-third he went
and climbed up on the roof. He meant
to clear the snow away that choked
his chimney up – of course he poked
his legs right through the tiles and snow
in tons fell on his bed below.
He has broken saucers, cups, and plates;
and eaten lots of chocolates;
he's dropped large boxes on my toes,
and trodden tin-soldiers flat in rows;

You need not believe all this!

You need!

he's over-wound engines and broken springs,
and mixed up different children's things;
he's thumbed new books and burst balloons
and scribbled lots of smudgy Runes
on my best paper, and wiped his feet
on scarves and hankies folded neat –
And yet he has been, on the whole,
a very kind and willing soul.
He's fetched and carried, counted, packed
and for a week has never slacked:

here hear!

I wish you wouldn't scribble
on my nice rhyme!

he's climbed the cellar-stairs at least
five thousand times – the Dear Old Beast!

Paksu sends love and Valkotukka –
They are still with me, and they don't look a
year older, but they're just a bit
more wise, and have a pinch more wit.

The GOBLINS, you'll be glad to hear,
have not been seen at all this year,
not near the Pole. But I am told,
they're moving south, and getting bold,
and coming back to many lands,
and making with their wicked hands
new mines and caves. But do not fear!
They'll hide away, when I appear.

Christmas Day

Now Christmas Day has come round again –
and poor North Polar Bear has got a bad pain!
They say he's swallowed a couple of pounds
of nuts without cracking the shells! It sounds
a Polarish sort of thing to do –
but that isn't all, between me and you:
he's eaten a ton of various goods
and recklessly mixed all his favourite foods,
honey with ham and turkey with treacle,
and pickles with milk. I think that a week'll
be needed to put the old bear on his feet.
And I mustn't forget his particular treat:
plum pudding with sausages and turkish delight
covered with cream and devoured at a bite!
And after this dish he stood on his head –
it's rather a wonder the poor fellow's not dead!

Absolute ROT:
I have not got
a pain in my pot.

Rude fellow!

I do not eat
turkey or meat:
I stick to the sweet.
Which is why
(as all know) I

smàs love

Paksu and Valkotukka —
They are still with me, & they don't look a
year older, but they're just a bit
more wise, & have a pinch more wit.

The GOBLINS, you'll be glad to hear,
have not been seen at all this year,
not near the Pole. But I am told,
they're moving South, and getting bold,
& coming back to many lands,
and making with their wicked hands
new mines & caves. But do not fear!
They'll hide away, when I appear.

Christmas Day. Postscript by Ilbereth.

Now Christmas Day has come round again —
and poor N.P.B. has got a bad pain!
They say he's swallowed a couple of pounds
of nuts without cracking the shells! It sounds
a Polarish sort of thing to do —
but that isn't all, between me and you:
he's eaten a ton of various goods
and recklessly mixed all his favourite foods,
honey with ham and turkey with treacle,
and pickles with milk. I think that a week'll
be needed to put the old bear on his feet.
And I mustn't forget his particular treat:
plum-pudding with sausages and Turkish delight
covered with cream and devoured at a bite!
And after this dish he stood on his head ———
its rather a wonder the poor fellow's not dead!

Absolute ROT:
I have not got
a pain in my pot.
I do not eat   Rude fellow!
turkey or meat:
I stick to the sweet.

Which is why
(as all know) I
am so sweet myself,
you thinuous elf!
Good by!

He means fatuous

no I don't   you're
not fat but
thin and silly

You know my friends too well to think
~~that~~ (al (g though they're rather rude with ink)
that there are redily pictrrels here!
We've had a very jolly year
(except for P.B's rusty nail);
but now this rhyme must catch the Mail —
a special messenger must go,
inspite of thickly falling snow,
or else this I won't get down to you
on Christmas day. It's half past two!
We've quite a ton of crackers still
to pull, and glasses still to fill!
Our love to you on this Noel —
and till the next one, fare you well!

Father Christmas.
P.F.
Ilbereth.
P Ꝺ ∨

**am so sweet myself,
you thinuous elf!
Goodby!**

He means fatuous

**No I don't, you're not fat,
but thin and silly.**

You know my friends too well to think
(although they're rather rude with ink)
that there are really quarrels here!
We've had a very jolly year
(except for Polar Bear's rusty nail);
but now this rhyme must catch the Mail –
a special messenger must go,
in spite of thickly falling snow,
or else this won't get down to you
on Christmas day. It's half past two!
We've quite a ton of crackers still
to pull, and glasses still to fill!
Our love to you on this Noel –
and till the next one, fare you well!

Father Christmas
Polar Bear
Ilbereth
Paksu and Valkotukka

My Dear P,

This is the last Beatrix Potter painting book I have got.
I don't believe they are making any more. I am sending it to you with love.

F.C.

Boxing Day 1938 On the feast of Stephen I have just
found it – and my letter never sent off. Most annoying.
Very sorry. But perhaps something after Christmas will
be rather nice?

Not my fault! PB Nor mine [can't decipher]

FC left them on his desk covered with wrapping paper

My dear P.

This is the last Beatrix Potter painting book I have got. I don't believe they are making any more. I am sending it to you with love.
FB

Boxing Day 1938   On the Feast of St Stephen
I have just found it — and my letter — never sent off. Most annoying.   Very sorry. But perhaps something after Christmas will be rather nice?

not my fault! FB *Nor mine — Hb.*

K left them on his desk covered with wrapping paper

1939

Cliff House,
NORTH POLE
December 24th 1939

My dear Priscilla

I am glad you managed to send me two letters
although you have been rather busy working. I hope
your Bingo family will have a jolly Christmas, and
behave themselves. Tell Billy – is not that the father's
name? – not to be so cross. They are not to quarrel
over the crackers I am sending.

I am very busy and things are very difficult this year
owing to this horrible war. Many of my messengers
have never come back. I haven't been able to do you
a very nice picture this year. It is supposed to show me
carrying things down our new path to the sleigh-sheds.
Paksu is in front with a torch looking most frightfully
pleased with himself (as usual). There is just a glimpse
(quite enough) of Polar Bear strolling along behind.
He is of course carrying nothing.

Cliff House
NORTH POLE
December 24th. 1939

My dear Priscilla

I am glad you managed to send me two letters although you have been rather busy working. I hope your Bingo family will have a jolly Christmas, & behave themselves. Tell Billy — is not that the father's name? — not to be so cross. They are not to quarrel over the crackers I am sending.

I am afraid there is no Basil coming. I have not got any small Bingos left! But I am sending a lovely clean aunt GILLY < which is short for Juliana > who will keep Milly in order I hope, or take her place if she does not improve. I hope all the other things are that you want.

I am very busy and things are very difficult this year owing to this horrible war. Many of my messengers have never come back. I haven't been able to do you a very nice picture this year. It is supposed to show me camping things down our new path to the sleigh-sheds

There have been no adventures here, and nothing funny has happened – and that is because Polar Bear has done hardly anything to "help", as he calls it, this year.

ROT!

I don't think he has been lazier than usual, but he has been not at all well. He ate some fish that disagreed with him last November and was afraid he might have to go to hospital in Greenland. But after living only on warm water for a fortnight he suddenly threw the glass and jug out of the window and decided to get better.

Paksu is in front with a torch looking most frightfully pleased with himself (as usual). There is just a glimpse (quite enough) of P.B. strolling along behind. He is of course carrying nothing.

There have been no adventures here, and nothing funnie has happened — and that is because P.B. has not done hardly anything "to help", as he calls it, this year. I don't think he has been lazier than usual, but he has been not at all well. He ate some fish that disagreed with him last November, and I was afraid he might have to go to hospital in Greenland. But after living only on warm water for a fortnight he suddenly threw the glass and jug out of the window and decided to get better.

He drew the trees in the picture. & I am afraid they are not very good. They look more like umbrellas! He bids he sends love to you and all your Bears. "Why don't you have Polar Cubs instead of Bingos & Koalas?" he says.

Give my love to Christopher and Michael and to John when you next write.

LOVE

from

Father Christmas

! ROT

BEST
PART
OF
IT

↓ WHY
NOT?
PB

He drew the trees in the picture, and I am afraid they are not very good.

Best part of it

They look more like umbrellas! Still he sends love to you and all your bears. "Why don't you have Polar Cubs instead of Bingos and Koalas?" he says.

Why not?

Give my love to Christopher and Michael and to John when you next write.

Love from Father Christmas.

DEAR P.   1940 · MONDAY
                                DEC 23
    GLAD TO FIND YOU ARE BACK!

message came on Sat that your house was
empty. Wos afrade you had gon without leaving
any address. Ar having verry DIFFICULT
time this year but ar doing my our best
THANK YOU for explaining about your room.
FR. sends love   ! Please excuse
blots Rather bizzy   Yours
                                P.B.

        MISS P.M.R.TOLKIEN
        20 NORTHMOOR
                RD.
        OXFORD

            ENGLAND

PB

168

1940

December 23rd 1940

Dear Priscilla

Glad to find you are back! Message came on Saturday that your house was empty. Wos afrade you had gon without leaving any address.

Ar having verry DIFFICULT time this year but ar doing my our best .

THANK YOU for explaining about your room. Father Christmas sends love! Please excuse blots. Rather bizzy.

Yours Polar Bear

Cliff House,
near North Pole
Christmas Eve 1940

My Dearest Priscilla

Just a short letter to wish you a very happy
Christmas. Please give my love to Christopher.
We are having rather a difficult time this year. This
horrible war is reducing all our stocks, and in so

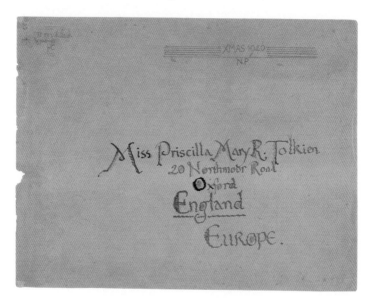

Cliff House.
near N. Pole
Christmas Eve
1940

My Dearest Priscilla.

Just a short letter to wish you a very happy Christmas. Please give my love to Christopher. We are having rather a difficult time this year. This horrible war is reducing all our stocks, and in so many countries children are living far from their homes. P.B. has had a very busy time trying to get our address-lists corrected. I am glad you are still at home. I wonder what you will think of my "picture". Penguins don't live at the "North Pole" you will say. I know they don't, but we have got some all the same. What you would call "evacuees" (I believe that's not a very nice word): except that they did not come here to escape the war, but to find it! They had heard such stories of the happenings up in the NORTH (including a quite untrue story that P.B. and all the Polar Cubs had been blown up, and that I had been captured by Goblins) that they swam all the way here to see if they could help me. Nearly 50 arrived. This is a picture of them dancing with their chiefs. They amused us enormously: they don't really help much, but are always playing funny dancing games, and trying to imitate the walk of P.B. and the Cubs ————— ƒ.

many countries children are living far from their homes. Polar Bear has had a very busy time trying to get our address-lists corrected. I am glad you are still at home!

I wonder what you will think of my picture. "Penguins don't live at the North Pole," you will say. I know they don't, but we have got some all the same. What you would call "evacuees", I believe (not a very nice word); except that they did not come here to escape the war, but to find it! They had heard such stories of the happenings up in the North (including a quite untrue story that Polar Bear and all the Polar Cubs had been blown up, and that I had been captured by Goblins) that they swam all the way here to see if they could help me. Nearly 50 arrived.

The picture is of Polar Bear dancing with their chiefs. They amuse us enormously: they don't really help much, but are always playing funny dancing games, and trying to imitate the walk of Polar Bear and the Cubs.

Very much love from your old friend,
Father Christmas

P.B. and all the Cubs are very well. They have really been very good this year & have hardly had time to get into any mischief.

I hope you will find most of the things that you wanted and am very sorry that I have no Cats Tongues left. But I have sent nearly all the books you asked for. I could not get the pamphlet in time. Perhaps your father could get them for you? All the same I hope your stocking will seem full!

VERY MUCH LOVE FROM YOUR
OLD FRIEND
Father Christmas.

1941

Cliff House,
near (stump of) North Pole
December 22nd, 1941

My Dearest Priscilla,

I am so glad you did not forget to write to me again
this year. The number of children who keep up with
me seems to be getting smaller: I expect it is because
of this horrible war, and that when it is over things
will improve again, and I shall be as busy as ever. But
at present so terribly many people have lost their
homes: or have left them; half the world seems in
the wrong place.

And even up here we have been having troubles.
I don't mean only with my stores: of course they are
getting low. They were already last year, and I have
not been able to fill them up, so that I have now to
send what I can instead of what is asked for. But worse
than that has happened.

I expect you remember that some years ago we had
trouble with the Goblins; and we thought we had
settled it. Well, it broke out again this autumn, worse

Cliff House
near (stump of) N. Pole
December 22nd 1941.

My Dearest Priscilla

I am so glad you did not forget to write
to me again this year. The number of children who keep up with me seems to be getting smaller.
I expect it is because of this horrible war, and that
when it is over things will improve again, and I shall
be as busy as ever. But at present so terribly
many people have lost their homes, or have
left them: half the world seems in the wrong place.
And even up here we have been having troubles.
I don't mean only with my stores; of course they
are getting low. They were already last year,
and I have not been able to fill them up, so that
I have now to send what I can instead of what is
asked for. But worse than that has happened.
I expect you remember that some years ago we had
trouble with the Goblins, and we thought we had
settled it. Well it broke out again this autumn worse
than it has been for centuries. We have had several
battles, and for a while my house was besieged. In
November it began to look likely that it would be
captured and all my goods, and that Christmas
Stockings would all remain empty all over the
world. Would not that have been a calamity?
It has not happened — and that is largely due to
the efforts of P.B. — but it was not until the
beginning of this month that I was able to

and out our messengers! I expect the Goblins thought that with so much war going on that was a fine chance to recapture the North. They must have been preparing for some years; and they made a huge new tunnel which had an _____ outlet (many miles away) just east in October that they suddenly came out in thousands. P.B. says there were at least a million, but that is his favourite big number. Johnny he was fast asleep at the time, and (was rather sleepy, myself). The weather was rather warm, for the time of the year, and Christmas seemed far away. There were only one or two elves about the place; and of course Polon and Valko (also fast asleep). The drums had all come away in the spring. Luckily Goblins cannot help getting up and beating on drums when they mean to fight; some all woke up in time, and our gates and doors barred and the windows shuttered. P.B. got on the roof and fired rockets into the Goblin hosts as they poured up the long reindeer-lane; but that did not stop them for long. We were soon surrounded. I have not time to tell you all the story. I had to blow three blasts on the great Horn (Windbeam) it hangs over the fire place from the hall, and if I have not told you about it before its because I have not had to blow it for ____ (There now! I was interrupted and it is now Christmas Eve, and I don't know when I shall get finished!) — over 4 hundred years; its sound carries as far as the North Wind blows. All the same it was three whole days before help came; dwarves, polarbears, and hundreds and hundreds of elves. They came up behind the Goblins; and P.B (really awake this time) rushed out with a blazing branch off the fire in each paw. He must have killed dozens of Goblins (he says a million). But there was a big battle down on the plain near the N. Pole in November, in which the Goblins brought hundreds of our companies out of their tunnels. We were driven back to the Cliff; and it was not until P.B and a party of his younger relatives crept out by night, and blew up the entrance to the new tunnels with nearly 100 lbs of gunpowder that we got the better of them — for the present. But bang went all the stuff for making fireworks and crackers (the cracking part) for some years. The N. Pole cracked and fell over for the second time; and we have not yet had time to mend it. ____ P.B is rather a hero (I hope he does not think so himself) But of course he is a very MAGICAL animal really, and Goblins can't do much to him, when he is awake and angry. I have seen their arrows bouncing off him and breaking. Well, that will give you some idea of events; and you will understand why. I have not had

THERE WER NO LESS 100000 000 OF EM.

I DO!

VB →

than it has been for centuries. We have had several battles, and for a while my house was besieged. In November it began to look likely that it would be captured and all my goods, and that Christmas Stockings would all remain empty all over the world.

Would not that have been a calamity? It has not happened – and that is largely due to the efforts of Polar Bear –

N.B. That's mee!

but it was not until the beginning of this month that I was able to send out any messengers! I expect the Goblins thought that with so much war going on this was a fine chance to recapture the North. They must have been preparing for some years; and they made a huge new tunnel which had an outlet many miles away.

It was early in October that they suddenly came out in thousands. Polar Bear says there were at least a million, but that is his favourite big number.

There wer at leest a hundred million.

Anyway, he was still fast asleep at the time, and I was rather drowsy myself; the weather was rather warm for the time of the year and Christmas seemed far away. There were only one or two elves about the place; and of course Paksu and Valkotukka (also fast asleep). The Penguins had all gone away in the spring.

Luckily Goblins cannot help yelling and beating on drums when they mean to fight; so we all woke up in time, and got the gates and doors barred and the windows shuttered. Polar Bear got on the roof and fired rockets into the Goblin hosts as they poured up the long reindeer-drive; but that did not stop them for long. We were soon surrounded.

I have not time to tell you all the story. I had to blow three blasts on the great Horn (Windbeam). It hangs over the fireplace in the hall, and if I have not told you about it before it is because I have not had to blow it for over 4 hundred years: its sound carries as far as the North Wind blows. All the same it was three whole days before help came: snowboys, polar bears, and hundreds and hundreds of elves.

They came up behind the Goblins: and Polar Bear (really awake this time) rushed out with a blazing branch off the fire in each paw. He must have killed dozens of Goblins (he says a million).

But there was a big battle down in the plain near the North Pole in November, in which the Goblins brought hundreds of new companies out of their tunnels. We were driven back to the Cliff, and it was not until Polar Bear and a party of his younger relatives crept out by night, and blew up the entrance to the new tunnels with nearly 100lbs of gunpowder that we got the better of them – for the present.

time to draw a picture this year — rather a pity, because there has been such exciting things to draw — and why I have not been able to collect the usual things for you, or even the very few that you asked for.

I am told that nearly all the Alison Uttely books have been burnt, and I could not find one of "Moldy Warp". I must try and get one for next time. I am sending you a few other books, which I hope you will like. There is not a great deal else, but I send you very much love.

I like to hear about your B. Bingo, but really I think he is too old and important to hang up stockings! But P.B seems to feel that any kind of bear is a relation. And he said to me "Leave it to me, old man (next I am afraid is what he often calls me): I will pack a perfectly beautiful selection for his Polaress (yes Polaress !)" So I shall try and bring the beautiful selection along : what it is, I don't know!

VERY MUCH LOVE FROM
your old friends

FATHER
CHRISTMAS
&
P.B.

Mr PMR Tolkien

England.

But bang went all the stuff for making fireworks
and crackers (the cracking part) for some years. The
North Pole cracked and fell over (for the second
time), and we have not yet had time to mend it. Polar
Bear is rather a hero (I hope he does not think so
himself)

I DO!

But of course he is a very MAGICAL animal really,

N.B.

and Goblins can't do much to him, when he is awake
and angry. I have seen their arrows bouncing off him
and breaking.

Well, that will give you some idea of events, and you
will understand why I have not had time to draw a
picture this year – rather a pity, because there have
been such exciting things to draw – and why I have
not been able to collect the usual things for you, or
even the very few that you asked for.

I am told that nearly all the Alison Uttley books have
been burnt, and I could not find one of 'Moldy Warp'.
I must try and get one for next time. I am sending you
a few other books, which I hope you will like. There is
not a great deal else, but I send you very much love.

I like to hear about your Bear Bingo, but really I think
he is too old and important to hang up stockings!

But Polar Bear seems to feel that any kind of bear is a relation. And he said to me, "Leave it to me, old man (that, I am afraid is what he often calls me): I will pack a perfectly beautiful selection for his Poliness (yes, Poliness!)". So I shall try and bring the 'beautiful selection' along: what it is, I don't know!

Very much love from your old friend Father Christmas and Polar Bear

1942

Cliff House,
North Pole
Christmas Eve 1942

My dear Priscilla,

Polar Bear tells me that he cannot find my letter from
you among this year's piles. I hope he has not lost any:
he is so untidy. Still I expect you have been very busy
this autumn at your new school.

I have had to guess what you would like. I think I
know fairly well, and luckily we are still pretty well off
for books and things of that sort. But really, you know,
I have never seen my stocks so low or my cellars so full
of empty places (as Polar Bear says).

I am hoping that I shall be able to replenish them
before long; though there is so much waste and
smashing going on that it makes me rather sad, and
anxious too. Deliveries too are more difficult than
ever this year with damaged houses and houseless
people and all the dreadful events going on in your
countries. Of course it is just as peaceful and merry in
my land as ever it was.*

Cliff House.
NORTH POLE.
CHRISTMAS 1942..

My dear Priscilla,

P.B. tells me that he cannot find any letter from you among this year's piles. I hope he has not lost any: he is so untidy. Still I expect you have been very busy this autumn at your new 5th cosy. I have had to guess what you would like. I think I know fairly well, and luckily we are still pretty well off for books and things of that sort. But really, you know, I have never seen my stocks so low or my cellars so full of empty places (as P.B. says, although he is not an Irish bear). I am hoping that I shall be able to replenish them before long; though there is so much waste and smashing going on that it makes me rather sad and anxious too. Deliveries too are more difficult than ever this year with damaged houses and houseless people and all the dreadful events going on in your countries. Of course it past as peaceful and merry in my land as ever it was. We had our snow early this year and then nice crisp frosty nights to keep it white and firm and bright starry days (no sun just now of course). I am giving as big a party tomorrow night as ever I did. polar cubs (P & T of course among them) and snowboys, and elves. We are having the Tree indoors this year — in the hall at the foot of the great staircase, and I hope P.B. does not fall down the stairs and crash into it after it is all decorated and lit up. I hope you will not mind my bringing this little letter along with your things tonight: I am short of messengers, as some have great trouble in finding people and have been away for days. Just now I caught P.B. in my pantry, and I am sure he had been to a cupboard. I do not know why. He has wrapped up a mysterious small parcel which he wants me to bring to you — "well not exactly to you (he said): she has got a bear too, as you ought to remember." Well my dear here is very much love from Father Christmas once more, and very good wishes for 1943 ♰.

* No battles at all this year. Quiet as quiet. I think the Goblins were really crushed this time. Windbeams is hanging over the mantlepiece and is quite dusty again, I am glad to say. But P.B. has spent lots of time this year making fresh gunpowder — just in case of trouble. He said "wouldn't that jub boy P.T.O.

We had our snow early this year and then nice crisp frosty nights to keep it white and firm, and bright starry 'days' (no sun just now of course).

I am giving as big a party tomorrow night as ever I did, polar cubs (Paksu and Valkotukka, of course, among them) and snowboys, and elves. We are having the Tree indoors this year – in the hall at the foot of the great staircase, and I hope Polar Bear does not fall down the stairs and crash into it after it is all decorated and lit up.

I hope you will not mind my bringing this little letter along with your things tonight: I am short of messengers, as some have great trouble in finding people and have been away for days. Just now I caught Polar Bear in my pantry, and I am sure he had been to a cupboard. I do not know why.

He has wrapped up a mysterious small parcel which he wants me to bring to you – well not exactly to you (he said): "She has got a bear too, as you ought to remember."

Well my dear here is very much love from Father Christmas once more, and very good wishes for 1943.

*No battles at all this year. Quiet as quiet. I think the Goblins were really crushed this time. Windbeam is hanging over the mantelpiece and is quite dusty again, I am glad to say. But Polar Bear has spent lots of time this year making fresh gunpowder – just in case of trouble. He said, "wouldn't that grubby little Billy like being here!" I don't know what he was talking about, unless it was about your bear: does he eat gunpowder?

You'll find out about the pantry! Ha! Ha! I know wot you like. Don't let that Billy Bear eat it all!
Love from Polar Bear.

Messige to Billy Bear from Polar Bear
Sorry I could not send you a really good bomb. All our powder has gone up in a big bang. You would have seen wot a really good exploashion is like. If yould been there.

Little Billy like being here!" I don't know what he was talking about, unless it was about your bear: does he eat gunpowder..?

LOVE FROM F.B YOU'LL FIND OUT
ABOUT THE PANTRY ! HA'HA' I KNOW WOT YOU
LIKE. DONT LET THAT B.B EAT IT ALL .

F.B.

Cliff House
N.P.
Christmas 1943.

My dear Priscilla

A very happy Christmas! I suppose
you will be hanging up your stocking just once
more: I hope so, for I have still a few little
things for you. After this I shall have to say "goodbye",
more or less: I mean, I shall not forget you. We
always keep the old numbers of our old friends and their
letters; and later on we hope to come back when they are
grown up and have houses of their own and children.
My messengers tell me that people call it
"grim" this year. I think they mean miserable: and so
it is, I fear, in very many places where I was specially
fond of going (like Germany); but I am very glad to
hear that you are still not really miserable. Don't be!
I am still very much alive, and shall come back again
soon, as merry as ever. There has been no damage in
my country; and though my stocks are running rather low
I hope soon to put that right.
P.B. — too "tired" to write himself (so he says) —
sends a special message to you: love and a hug! He
says: do ask if she still has a bear called
Billy Billy, or something like that; or is he worn out?
Give my love to the others: John & Michael &
Chris topher — and of course to all your pets that
you used to tell me about.

P.T.O.

I AM
REELY

1943

Cliff House,
North Pole,
Christmas 1943

My dear Priscilla

A very happy Christmas! I suppose you will be hanging
up your stocking just once more: I hope so for I have
still a few little things for you. After this I shall have
to say "goodbye", more or less: I mean, I shall not
forget you. We always keep the old numbers of our
old friends, and their letters; and later on we hope to
come back when they are grown up and have
houses of their own and children.

My messengers tell me that people call it "grim" this
year. I think they mean miserable: and so it is, I fear,
in very many places where I was specially fond of going;
but I am very glad to hear that you are still not really
miserable. Don't be! I am still very much alive, and
shall come back again soon, as merry as ever. There has
been no damage in my country; and though my stocks
are running rather low I hope soon to put that right.

Polar Bear – too "tired" to write himself (so he says) –

I am, reely

sends a special message to you: love and a hug! He
says: do ask if she still has a bear called Silly Billy, or
something like that; or is he worn out?

Give my love to the others: John and Michael and
Christopher – and of course to all your pets that you
used to tell me about. Polar Bear and all the Cubs are
very well. They have really been very good this year
and have hardly had time to get into any mischief.

I hope you will find most of the things that you
wanted and I am very sorry that I have no 'Cats'
Tongues' left. But I have sent nearly all the books you
asked for. I hope your stocking will seem full!

Very much love from your old friend,
Father Christmas.

As I have not got very many of the things you usually want, I am sending you some nice bright clean money — I have lots of of that (more than you have, I expect, but is not very much use to me, perhaps it will be to you). You might find it useful to buy a book with that you really want Very much love from your old friend

Father Christmas.

X ^A MERRY CHRISTMAS.